THE INLARI SAGAS
INTERSPECIES
VOLUME I

M. J. KELLEY
DANA LEIPOLD

ELAINE CHAO
WOELF DIETRICH

kōsa press

Published by
Kōsa Press
www.kosapress.com
Kosa Media, LLC
San Francisco, CA, USA, & Hastings, Hawke's Bay, New Zealand
For more information, please contact the publisher at info@kosapress.com.

Edited by Ally Bishop
Cover design by Piotr Foksowicz
Book layout by Creative Kook Designs
ISBN: 978-0-9941240-0-5

First Edition: August 2016

10 9 8 7 6 5 4 3 2 1

CONTENTS

FOREWORD

FIRST MET SAMMY Davis, Junior, when I was nine. At the edge of the kitchen counter, he waited, a gray house lizard—what we in the Philippines called *butiki*. No bigger than my father's index finger, half of him was a thin, twitching tail that tapered to a point.

Sammy Davis was a similar specimen of *Hemidactylus frenatus* that my mother and father discovered long ago in their first apartment near España Boulevard in Manila. He had kept the moths and mosquitos at bay, and so they'd tolerated, then befriended him.

Now, several years later, my father approached Junior, making a series of clicks with his tongue, his hand outstretched with a pinch of boiled rice. My mother continued nibbling at her steamed chicken while my seven-year-old brother watched with a kind of stunned, frightened look in his eyes.

Still clicking—a quick *click-click-click*, pause, repeat—my father carefully set down the pinch of rice about two inches away, while the lizard watched with rotating eyes.

It took about half a minute while the lizard twitched his tail, swung his head first this way, then that—before he darted forward and snapped up the rice, swallowed, then darted away down the vertical side of the counter.

Triumphant, my father offered another pinch of rice.

Click-click-click.

Junior poked his head over the edge, scrambled to the rice, and gobbled it up.

Click-click-click.

Koko, a lowland gorilla trained by Dr. Penny Patterson, is said to comprehend over one thousand signs from American Sign Language and to understand and respond to a spoken vocabulary of over two thousand English words. Beyond that, Koko is reported to have invented her own signs to communicate new thoughts: for example, describing a ring by combining "finger" and "bracelet" into the new word "finger-bracelet."

Kanzi, a bonobo, has been using a specialized keyboard with symbols on the keys to communicate with the team of primatologist Sue Savage-Rumbaugh, using a vocabulary of six hundred words.

Alex, an African Grey, was shown by Dr. Irene Pepperberg to understand over a hundred English words and could identify various colors and shapes.

A controversial project in the 1970s saw a baby chimpanzee named Neam Chimpsky—"Nim," for short—taken from his mother just days after birth at a primate research center. Behavioral psychologist Herbert Terrace aimed to raise Nim as a human child, placing him with human families who strove to teach him a form of American Sign Language. Despite a sad end, when researchers attempted to re-integrate him unsuccessfully with other chimpanzees, Nim learned to sign in three- and four-word sentences:

Apple me eat.
Drink me Nim.
Finish hug Nim.
Give me eat.
Hug me Nim.
Tickle me Nim.
Yogurt Nim eat.
Banana eat me Nim.
Me eat drink more.
Tickle me Nim play.

IN A NASA-FUNDED EXPERIMENT WITH A BOTTLENOSE DOLPHIN named Peter, neuroscientist John C. Lilly tried to prove his theory that dolphins could learn language via constant human contact. Over ten weeks, Margaret Howe, his research assistant, spent day and night with Peter.

Dolphins can make human-sounding noises via their blowholes, and Margaret's goal was for Peter to mimic sounds that he heard.

Over time, Peter could pronounce a rough version of several words, including "hello," "we," "one," "triangle," "diamond," and "ball." His favorites:

Hello, Margaret
Play, play, play

Disturbingly, Peter got emotionally attached to and aggressive with Margaret, circling around her, nibbling her, and jamming himself against her legs. The behavior escalated, and he was quickly re-instated with other dolphins until he had calmed down enough to be re-introduced to Margaret.

Unfortunately, after ten weeks, funding for the project ended, and Peter was shipped to another lab. Without Margaret, he apparently lost the will to live and refused to breathe, sinking to the bottom of his tank in what might be understood as suicide.

MONTHS LATER, I'M ALONE IN THE KITCHEN WHEN I HEAR A clicking beside me.

There is Junior, his eyes two quivering balls of black, his tail flicking, right in the middle of the table.

Click-click-click.

I throw a rice grain at him, and he runs forward, catching it in his mouth and swallowing. I follow with several more.

Click-click.

Two clicks means "I'm done." He twitches his tail one more time, turns, and is gone.

ON AUGUST 15, 1977, ASTRONOMER JERRY EHMAN WAS EXAMINING data from Ohio State University's radio telescope, part of the Search for Extraterrestrial Intelligence (SETI) project. He saw an anomaly in the data from the direction of the constellation Sagittarius in the 1.43GHz frequency. Most scientists agree that would be the most likely frequency an alien civilization would use to broadcast a signal. It was so amazing that Ehman circled it and wrote "Wow!" in the margin of the print-out. Up until then, the signal had resisted all explanation. The signal's strength was represented on a scale of thirty-six intensity levels by the numerals 0-9, then A-Z. The 72-second signal formed a perfect bell curve:

6EQUJ5

We are here.

OUT THERE, BEYOND THE FURTHEST ARMS OF OUR GALAXY, OUR radio telescopes broadcast our own signals, our hopes and dreams, in a language we hope someone will understand.

Our spacecraft bear plaques engraved with drawings and symbols of ourselves in a form we hope someone will decipher.

And we listen, straining to hear beyond the noise of supernovae and neutron stars, to ascertain if there is indeed somebody out there.

CLICK-CLICK-CLICK.

Samuel Peralta, PhD
Physicist and creator of *The Future Chronicles*

TIMELINE

BFC – Before First Contact on Earth

AFC – After First Contact on Earth

2 Million Years BFC

Inlarah, last known original inlari world, destroyed by the Rordorah.

1.75 Million Years BFC

Landing on Lenti, first post-Inlarah planet. Rordorah destroys it.

975 Thousand Years BFC

Landing on Nep, the sixth post-Inlarah planet. Rordorah destroys it.

750 Thousand Years BFC

The Great Split: the fleet separates.

600 Thousand Years BFC

First contact with the hostile species boleeron on Feralu.

121 Years BFC

Again, the boleeron attack Naru, the eighth post-Inlarah planet.

2 Years BFC

Space-time warping technology is achieved for the first time.

0 YEAR
First contact: the inlari arrive on Earth.

1 YEAR AFC
Inlari strike a pact with the nations of Earth to trade technology for refuge.

20 YEARS AFC
Some of the nations of Earth request that the inlari distribute technology fairly or leave.

43 YEARS AFC
Inlari accepted into Australia and New Zealand and most migrate there.

50-58 YEARS AFC
The Great Earth/Inlari War.

58 YEARS AFC
Weapons of mass destruction ravage most of Earth's surface. Starships and warp technology are lost, as well as other technologies.

61 YEARS AFC
Inlari extremists take over in New Zealand and make arrangements to enslave the human population.

62 YEARS AFC
Naven expels all inlari from its walls and isolates itself from the world.

INTRODUCTION

FIFTY YEARS AFTER first contact with the inlari, war ravaged the Earth, leaving New Zealand and Australia the victors and survivors but at a devastating cost. Soon after the war, an extremist group of inlari seized New Zealand's North and South Islands, enslaving the human population in worship of their ancient galactic past. Australia remains fractured. City-states and townships govern small territories and uphold, or evade, justice. Inlari slaving parties raid human populations. Technology is scarce and hoarded by the powerful. Mass communications are all but extinct. Disparate factions maraud the last habitable land masses, and vast tent encampments swell with the hopeless and desperate. Yet there are those who still search for meaning, for a way to rebuild and reestablish the great brotherhood and the golden era of interspecies collaboration. Some still seek peace and unity—and with them, hope lives on.

THE MEMORIAM

M. J. KELLEY

101 YEARS AFC

THE NEEDLE HOVERED above Kene's face, the point aiming down between his budding horns.

A needle as long as he was tall.

Kene pressed against the restraints that held him in a kneeling position, his hands shackled on either side of him, his head in a metallic vise-like helmet with an opening for the needle. Behind the approaching syringe, controlling its trajectory with a machine, stood Broon, tall and skinny with thick horns the color of yellow clouds. Broon focused on maneuvering the long arc of the needle.

As the metal penetrated his scalp, crackling resounded inside his skull, like the echo of splitting wood. He winced, every muscle rebelling against the intrusion. Then he stiffened, bringing his tight and throbbing limbs under control, afraid his reactionary movements would scramble his brains as the needle slid deeper inside.

"You'll be fine," Broon murmured. "Stay calm."

A hum vibrated in Kene's ears, and he tried to say something. But his voice faded as the needle punctured his mind. Drool filled his mouth and dripped over his lips.

Fear entwined memories of his family.

"We're so proud of you." Mother pressed her face close to his and whispered, "You'll do great things. You've been chosen."

His father stood above him: "Succeed or fail, you'll always have a home here."

Broon informed Kene and his family: "He's special, a genetic profile of one in a million. But many tests still remain."

And then Kene followed Broon away from his home as his family watched.

Nine when he left, he'd been chosen alongside forty other children. All potential replacements for the *Memoriam,* a powerful, mythic figure within his people's society and government. A year of testing with the other children earned him this room, this last test.

The syringe tunneled into Kene's brain. Broon wavered above him, behind the apparatus's outstretched arm, and glowed with a rainbow aura that had not been there before. Kene tried to blink it away, but with every eyelid flutter the illusion strengthened, overpowering any sense of reality as his surroundings melted. Colorful spirals swarmed outward from Broon's face.

Kene's hands and feet tingled to numbness, and mucus dripped from his nose, thick saliva from his mouth. The black robotic arm holding the syringe extended toward him, driving the needle deeper. The room twisted and warped, and exhaustion permeated his limbs. If it weren't for the helmet holding him erect, he would have collapsed onto the floor.

"The test is positive." Broon's words throbbed into Kene's awareness.

Positive?

He would not be going home.

The thought dissipated as the unreality caused by the syringe overwhelmed his senses. He could no longer tell whether his eyes were open or closed, could no longer sense his body or anyone else in the room. A desperate part of his mind searched for a dream or fantasy to soothe and distract himself from the trauma, but his brain formed no pictures, recalled no memories. No dreams came. So, too, his fear dwindled, evaporating like steam. And Kene's awareness blinked out.

AFTER A LONG SEA VOYAGE, BROON DELIVERED KENE TO A WIND-swept beach on the South Island, far from his North Island home of Lakarta. On a wave-carved embankment, he presented Kene before two males, seaside hills rising behind them.

One figure wore the black uniform of a *Parhata* soldier. He stood tall and wide-chested with skinny, ridged horns advancing from his scalp.

The other figure stood shorter than Broon and the *Parhata,* his horns not the lattice-type or the skinny type nor the kind that extend from the sides of his face—rather, they grew thick and tall, jutting from the upper sides of his skull and reaching back behind his head like upturned tusks. A simple black garment draped his narrow frame.

Broon touched Kene's shoulder. "This is Palor. And the *Parhata* is called Deliz; he's charged with the *Memoriam*'s protection."

Palor tilted his head down toward Kene, compassion curving one side of his mouth. "He's older than I expected."

"He passed the test," Broon said.

"I see the scar." Palor kneeled down to meet Kene's gaze and then pointed to a puckered dot of flesh between his own long horns. "I am like you."

Palor's inviting face encouraged Kene to relax. The need to impress this *Memoriam* swelled inside him, but his anxiety over making a mistake and his longing for home suppressed the urge. He said nothing, his gaze falling to the sand.

Palor stood, turning to the high hills in the distance. "We should depart."

Broon said his goodbyes. And then Kene, Palor, and Deliz slogged onward parallel to the shore. The waves' rhythmic crashing resounded inside Kene as he watched the small curling swells impact the sand and dissolve to milky foam. On this south island, nature seemed to rule, as no roads carved the hillsides. No homes mounted the curved peaks.

The light had faded by the time they reached a break in the shoreline where a river emptied into the sea. Arriving at the river's mouth, they turned inland. Kene's legs blazed from trouncing through the sand. They strode onward, a dusky, pink hue all around as the sun set behind them and the river rushed by far below. Ahead, a dingy encampment clung to a valley's edge, nestled between the hill's base and the river. Thin smoke rose from between plastic habitats and oddly shaped lodges. Beyond the encampment's hodgepodge, the grass relinquished the land to trees, which lined only the fringes of the valley.

At the farthest end, the fields abruptly ended, but not at trees. Silver towers rose from behind a fortified wall—a city, with no roads going in or out. The monolithic buildings didn't belong against the snowcapped mountains yet, there they endured, as if nature had evolved around them, the lush surroundings exalting the city's symmetry in the vanishing light, interrupting the landscape like an afterimage from a dream.

"The city is Naven." Palor's voice startled Kene, who shivered at his words. "It's an old city, built eighty or so years ago, long before the Great Earth War." Palor stared out at the darkening valley. "We'll spend a long time here together."

When they reached the small camp, Deliz, who had been silent during the journey, said goodbye, bowed to Palor, and walked off.

Palor guided Kene through the mud-riddled paths snaking between the encampment's plastic canvas homes. Exhausted, Kene's hands dangled like weights at his sides, fatigue suppressing his apprehension of being in a new place.

Some inhabitants toted water from the river in plastic canisters; fires snapped and sputtered, ready for cooking; old emergency habitats, left over from the Great Earth War, offered shelter. No one wore armor or carried weapons.

Kene sensed an absence in the scenery, something missing. "Where are all the machines? The power?" The encampment seemed impoverished, a bizarre contrast to the luxury he expected from Palor's position.

Palor glanced at him and then he pointed at the darkening city, the spires reflecting the sunset's reddish violet hues. "Here, we obey Naven's laws. Naven is a human city. They're purists. Isolationists. A human stronghold in the midst of our territory. Naven demands that no inlari shall come within fourteen miles of the city with any machines, weapons, or digital technology. Nothing that runs on electricity shall enter the city's perimeter. No threats, you see. Otherwise, the penalty is death." He took in a deep breath. "We obey their laws. We're guests in Naven's shadow."

Kene scanned the muddy trails between the homes: tunic-clad figures scrubbed elaborately woven cloths in an oblong wash basin carved from a tree trunk; long wooden flutes, hollowed to hold water, stood erect near the dark entryways of homes; green metal sheets abutting the nearest fire, sizzled with strange smells as a short male carefully positioned smoking fish and mussels on them.

"Hungry? If there's one name you should memorize, it's Talib. Our cook." Palor gestured to the short male.

Kene glanced at Talib and then turned to Palor. "Why are we here?"

"Expected the lavishness of a Lakarta palace? The halls of the Parliament?" Palor chuckled. "We're here to create peace with the humans so that your family will remain safe. So that all of us can be secure." Palor crouched down. "You're here to study diplomacy, to learn the remaining human languages. And to *remember.*" He gave Kene's shoulders a gentle shake. "I know how hard it is to leave your home and your family. I know because I was once like you." Palor rose again.

"We helped them build it, you know," Palor continued. "Inlaris and humans constructed Naven together. There were many cities like it. Its birth represented a union of our two species. But after slavery was reinstituted on Lakarta and all the humans on these isles were rounded up as property, Naven's free humans forcibly ejected us. Can't blame them really. Now, it's the ultimate symbol for human resistance. All humans look to Naven. That's why peace must begin here." Palor adjusted his robe. "The city survived the

Great Earth War and has defended against our attacks ever since. It has self-sustained all this time. Much of the technology we lost in the war may still live on inside those walls. They have everything they need—for now."

"Do they have starships?"

Palor laughed. "No. Those are all gone I'm afraid, along with the infrastructure to build them—to build much of the grandeur we once enjoyed. The war made sure of that." Palor lifted the plastic canvas flap to his habitat.

Before they entered, Kene gazed once more upon Naven. The encroaching night tarnished the sterling spires to a blackish gray.

"Welcome to Anthro," Palor's voice intoned from behind him. "An embassy to the last free city humans have on these isles of New Zealand."

KENE AWOKE TO FOOTSTEPS OUTSIDE AND CASUAL MURMURING, preparations for the day. The small home held two beds, a desk, and a stool made from a tree trunk. Lavish rugs hid the dirt floor with their intricate violets and greens.

"I have something special to show you today." Palor stretched his legs.

Kene hurried out of bed, excitement and nervousness squirming together inside him.

He trailed Palor through the encampment, winding between the habitats until only the forest lay before them to the left and the grasslands to the right. They walked in silence, their footfalls crushing the tall, thin blades until Palor stopped and turned to Kene.

"You'll become a *Memoriam* like me. You'll join an ancient

order, one that flourished before our arrival on Earth. Now, for all but a few, we're forgotten figures shrouded in myth and legend." Palor smashed the grass down around them, creating a circle. "*Memoriams* imprint the memories of the old and dying, copying them to our own minds. We have the power to recall these memories at will. We learn from memories. They guide us and help us guide our leaders—and our species."

Palor sat on the flattened grass and gestured for Kene to join him. "It's not mystical or a kind of magic, but a harnessing of the mind through an ancient technology. You and I have the ability to experience memory with our brains' perceptual segments. So we smell, hear, feel, see, taste, and know. You don't have to understand, yet." He pulled the satchel around from his back. "We must start slowly, only a few memories at a time. It will be painful. Draining. After today, you'll be exhausted. We always start with pain. But you'll learn to cope with the memories and to process these lives. We will imprint every day. And before I die, you'll have all my memories, the ones I created and those passed to me."

Palor took out a long, pearly metal rod, shaped oddly with a bulge in the middle, like a strange animal bone. "The *kin*. Take one end and press it to your scar. I focus on a memory, the *kin* records my impulses, then stimulates the same impulses in your brain, copying the memory."

Kene guided the other end of the *kin* to his scar. He could feel Palor's breath on his face as they leaned toward one another. The *kin's* surface shifted like gray paint mixed with water, then colors flamed across it, shining outward in vibrant curves.

"Close your eyes."

Kene obeyed. Needles pricked his skin, proceeded by the sensation of falling. He tried to open his eyes but couldn't. Darkness reigned, but then lights flickered in the distance. Kene drifted, his limbs floating, weightless, as if he'd been released from gravity. The lights formed familiar specks, and then the void erupted with stars.

Incandescent lines zipped by as the stars shifted, folding into streams. Soon, the only brightness left was a small yellow star.

Kene entered the star's system, shooting by gas and ice giants. *Inlar*—the thought dropped into his mind unprompted. *Tiny Inlar, last of our known stars.* A small planet flew into view—*Inlarah*—wrapped in blackness, the surface fractured with molten cracks. Leaving the atmosphere, starships in the thousands blasted into space with a glitter of pulsing engines like diamond dust ejected against an inky backdrop.

The vision of the fleet escaping Inlarah faded, transitioning to a different memory. Now from inside a ship—*the Essariah*—Kene looked back at Inlar as the globe dimmed, reds and blues vanishing, the surface consumed by the darkness.

The *Essariah's* halls lay before him like bleached bones, hollowed out and tunnel-shaped, the ceiling, walls, and floor forming an oval. Elliptical light fixtures corrugated the passageways, their luminosity subduing all in blue. When Kene peered at the storage bay from one of the many balconies encircling the room, he saw a netted latticework of suspended beds occupying every cubic meter of space. Immense, with gradually curving walls, the bay was the largest part of the ship. The refugees hung in silent packs among the netting, a mélange of dangling bodies, hundreds caught in the elaborate municipality like insects in a layered web.

This is where they would live and sleep. This is where they would die.

Generations would call this home.

And with that realization glimmering in him, the bay faded, and the field blurred back into Kene's vision, grass blowing all around him from a light wind. He blinked, barely able to keep his eyes open. The imprint had ended, but his arms and legs refused to awaken.

He had no strength to walk, so Palor carried him back.

"Two million years have passed since we left that planet," Palor whispered. "Yet the memories of the evacuation are still recalled, still re-lived, by you and me. Inlaris should never forget. And the *Memoriam* remembers for all. We remember for a species."

Kene, exhausted from the imprint, spent the rest of the day in bed. The *Essariah*'s suspended bodies appeared to him unbidden, capturing his senses, forcing him to see, to experience. He traversed between the living world and the memory realm in spontaneous flashes, as if these memories controlled his mind and body— the dead lashing out at him, uninvited, their feelings, thoughts, tragedies, hopes, and failures bubbling up in his mind like lethal gases on a noxious ocean.

He'd not seen his family in a year, and now, more than ever, his mind consumed by the dead's memories, he yearned for home.

The following day, Kene lay still, ignoring Palor's waking movements.

"Rise. I have more to give you."

He found the idea of accepting more memories intolerable, worse than the year of testing he'd undergone. Worse than even the needle, because these memories would never leave him alone.

"Get up."

"No!" Kene curled into a tight ball.

"I was worried about this." Palor stood over him. "You're too old. Too undisciplined."

He glared at Palor, his anger driven by fear rather than conviction.

Palor sighed and sat on his bed. A long silence ensued, as if he needed to collect his thoughts. "*Memoriams* live our lives mindful that our memories will be passed on. Each *Memoriam,* before his or her life ends, attempts to accomplish at least one task that no other ever has, adding some new experience to the *remembrance* for future generations of our order. We call this our *remari.* My *remari* is peace with Naven. I left the leadership council, left the Parliament to come here. It's been five years in this valley, and Naven is finally speaking, finally extending graciousness to us. No one else could do this. No one else was willing. Even leaders like Alteiri deny the necessity for peace. They favor slavery and the old ways, as if the exodus has taught us nothing. But I persist. As you will persist." Palor stood. "Peace—you think I'd risk that because you're tired? Because you can't manage after *one* imprint? Do we give up two million years of memories because you won't rise from bed? Those memories won't die with me. I can promise you that."

Kene hugged himself tighter.

"Discipline is the *Memoriam's* foundation."

"I don't want to see any more." Kene pushed out the words.

Palor grabbed a large, smooth walking stick that leaned against the canvas wall. Kene heard the slap before the impact rippled through his body.

Palor raised the staff again.

"No!" Kene cried. He braced for another strike, and it came with more force, leaving him breathless. He struggled to inhale as his tears dampened the rugs.

"Get up."

Kene struggled to his feet, the fear of a third strike motivating him, and, reluctantly, he followed Palor out of the encampment.

EVERY DAY, PALOR LED KENE TO THE FIELD, AND A NEW SET OF memories filled his mind. The *kin* pressed into his scar, he closed his eyes and witnessed the valley before Naven's construction, green with blowing wild grasses, then full of his people and humans. Starships drifted overhead, lowering beams and supply crates on thick, metal lines. Excavation pits gaped, brown and perfectly circular, as drills plumbed their depths for bedrock. White discs half a mile across hovered above the site, lifting beams into place—the origin of Naven's towers. As the sun reached its apex, the discs cast spherical shadows over the naked columns, innards bare to the world.

Then the memory faded into another—a refugee—pulled from her home in Naven by human soldiers, marched out of the city walls with weapons aimed at her back. She was one among thousands of his people, those who helped build the city, expelled forever.

Kene died forty times as he tried to breach the city's walls. At night, sounds like thunder boomed across the valley as lights strobed overhead. Naven bloomed with arcing flares and flying sparks, with missiles streaming into the surrounding forests and fields like some giant night flower spreading its deadly pollen and barbs.

Orange flames speckled the fields and forests around the city as explosions hissed and popped overhead. Before Naven's wall, an army of berserkers fell, their heads exploding into bloody mists, their tusks splintering into shrapnel. Volley after volley from the small gun turrets in the wall lay waste to all around him until he, too, lay dying on the scorched land, the grass now gone, his last memory a *Memoriam* hovering over him.

He watched from the rear as a long procession of soldiers marched through wooded hills toward the sea. The young Theede Fendo—somewhere at the head of his army, leading the retreat from Naven's valley—had failed to retake the human city that audaciously persisted on the land he commanded.

Failed just like his father before him.

When Kene refused to rise from his bed, refused to witness another starship explode into the eternal night—refused to be another child maimed by the boleerons, another soldier gunned down in front of Naven's walls, a slaver capturing humans when his people usurped New Zealand, a young female after Inlarah's destruction, placed in a cryotube by her mother, never to see her family again—all visited prior to death, their last vision a *Memoriam* placing a *kin* between their horns.

When he refused to take any more, refused to follow Palor into that dreadful field, Palor would say, "You're seeing, experiencing things no child should ever witness, just as I did. Your knowledge is adult knowledge. But we must continue. In time, you'll learn how to manage all this. To order it. And it will change you. But first, we always begin with pain."

"No."

And Palor would raise his staff again, and Kene would wince, preparing himself for yet another strike. *I'm failing,* Kene would think. *This is too much.*

In the afternoons, a human named Marcus would sometimes arrive from Naven, bringing Palor an electronic slate on which he could read and respond to messages. Marcus looked upon Kene with a dull expression. Kene thought he saw pity in Marcus's gaze, but he couldn't be sure. Marcus had a daughter, Alta, who occasionally accompanied him. One time, Alta took his hand and opening it, placed a token there. The humans had etched the city's towers into the token's metal. Unable to understand each other, they ran together in the nearby forest, playing a game of sorts, until Marcus grabbed Alta's arm and dragged her, flailing and squealing, back to a hovercraft. After many of these play sessions, Alta stopped accompanying Marcus. Kene never discovered why.

The full impact of his isolation dragged Kene down, his loneliness coexisting with memories he longed to forget. At night, before sleep took him, he would finger the token in his pocket, remembering his brief friend's smile.

I can't do this anymore.

Leaving Kene in Deliz or Talib's care, Palor would accompany Marcus to peace negotiations just outside Naven's walls. He would return late at night, exhausted from the talks, falling asleep quickly. On a night that Palor returned late, Kene had to wait only a few minutes until his mentor's rhythmic breathing punctuated the quiet tent. Kene crept quietly from his bed and confiscated water flutes and food packs from a box outside the tent's entrance. He removed the *kin* and other *Memoriam* tools from Palor's satchel and placed the food and water inside, leaving the tools behind.

Outside, some of the cooking fires still smoldered, their embers a fading glow. While Anthro slept, Kene weaved between the habitats, his feet bare, careful not to break twigs or trip. He made his way along the river trail, the rushing water concealing any noise. He reached the shore and then trailed the edge toward where the transport had originally dropped him off. The light of stars and moon filtered, the night paled by sea fog, no dark feature of land or water offered itself to his eyes. The crashing waves and fanning foam slushed somewhere off to the left, rinsing the sand in sound only. Could the water wash him too? Rinse away the memories wrapped around his mind? No. The memories could not be suppressed. Could not diminish with time. They only strengthened their fierce resolve to last, and last within him. But the ocean gave him hope.

The sun emerged like a slow epiphany, haze evaporating as pink rays cut through the mist, linear tendrils revealing the ocean and wind-carved embankment ahead. Hope tingled along his skin as a watercraft drew near, similar to the one that had brought him here.

Figures stood on the embankment, dark lines against the corroded sea hills. He ran toward them, afraid to miss the approaching carrier, which rode a wave to shore and hovered over the sand to a stop. People exited the craft through vertical doors, and Kene ran until one of the figures approaching the carrier spotted him.

"Hey!" The figure waved at Kene.

It was Deliz.

The tall soldier skidded down the embankment. Kene just stood there, defeated by his fatigue and the universe's betrayal.

"Going on a trip?" Deliz laughed and took his hand. But Kene barely heard him, the tears cold against his face, now indiscernible from the seawater collecting on his bony cheeks. He had no fight left in him, no urge to run. Why escape now when Deliz would only overpower him?

"I've been waiting for new arrivals. But I didn't know I was waiting for you as well." Two females slogged up behind Deliz.

They introduced themselves as Elma, a medic, and Ro, another *Parhata* soldier.

"It's an escaped *Memoriam*." Deliz gestured to Kene, and the females chuckled.

Kene, already feeling the crack of Palor's staff on his back, soured with the mockery.

They began the trek over the sand to the river's mouth.

"Is it so painful?" Ro smiled at him. "Is it so bad you have to run away?" Her ankles chimed with bracelets of tinkling metals, little bells pervading her every step with music. Long metal sheets in thin rectangles encircled her neck. Her horns were thick, their roots starting just above her cheeks and rising high over her head, and her face, although rigid, seemed young to Kene—a female of twenty-five Earth years or so.

Kene nodded. *How could she ever understand?*

But then, looking over her face, he discovered the puckered, wrinkled flesh that formed a fingerprint-sized circle between her horns, just like his.

THAT NIGHT, KENE PACED INSIDE PALOR'S HABITAT, WAITING FOR him to return from Naven, waiting to receive his punishment.

Waiting to confront Palor's lies.

"You must learn not to run away again." Palor stepped through the plastic entry flaps. "I'm almost too weary to punish you." He lifted his staff from the place by the desk.

"You lied."

Palor hesitated, grasping the long, heavy stick as if struck by the words.

Kene sensed the power of what he'd said. "Liar," he repeated.

Palor leaned the stick back against the plastic wall and sat on his bed, staring at Kene with confusion. "I've been nothing but honest with you."

"Then who is she?"

"Who?"

"You said you were the last. That we were special."

"I am. We are."

"What about the female with the scar?"

Palor gazed down at Kene. "Ro is here?" Palor sighed heavily and slouched forward against one of the habitat's supports. "She's not a *Memoriam*. She was my mentor's last disciple. He took her in after I completed my training. She was too old, like you. But Loy was stubborn. He took her in; however, the memories he gave her vanished from his own mind. Loy tried to retrieve them from her, but he found that she had forgotten them too."

"You said that was impossible."

"For you and me. For real *Memoriams,* unless we imprint with a *Fugue* like Ro. That's what she is. It's not her fault. Her kind are rare. But they do materialize from time to time. We still don't know how to test for them."

Palor leaned closer to Kene, gazing intently at him. "*Fugues* can't control what they remember and what they forget. And what you give a *Fugue,* you lose. Loy thought his *remari*, his great contribution, was fixing the *Fugue* and being the first ever to do so. He thought he could teach her control. When he discovered he couldn't, he did something worse."

Palor slid off his bed, placing his knees on the ground. "These memories we carry, you've not seen the worst. For some, the worst can drain you, make you age. Loy, at the end of his life, thought he could rid himself of the worst and extend his final years. He became obsessed and used the *Fugue* to forget. He plunged all his worst, most damaging memories into her, telling her, 'We begin with pain,' telling her she was still being instructed. He evacuated from his mind all the pain he'd come to bear over his lifetime."

After a long silence, Kene whispered, "What happened to him?"

Palor's gaze met Kene's. "He died of old age anyway, never completing the *Fugue's* training, never fixing her, never extending his own life, no *remari* devoted to the *remembrance*. Ro sought an apprenticeship from me, but I turned her away. There is no known way to transform a *Fugue*."

Palor placed his hand on Kene's shoulder, and his mouth curved to a smile, yet, one that only expressed sadness. "She's a soldier now. Deliz requested another *Parhata* to help protect us, and they sent her. Come to spy on me. Probably for Alteiri or one of the other commanders. My authority does not include the *Parhata*. It doesn't matter. Let her spy and report. Our progress is too far along." Palor pushed down on Kene's shoulders, guiding him to a sitting position. "I've never had children. I only have the memories of parents, and memories won't always produce the right actions. I can give you memories of how I learned the human languages, but that will not enable you to speak them. I don't know why, but it doesn't work that way." Palor lifted the *kin* from the ground. "Have I lied to you?"

Kene didn't know what to say.

"I trust you, Kene. I have to trust you more than anyone living." He pressed the *kin* against his own scar, closing his eyes. "I now know what to show you."

Kene leaned forward as if in a trance. He closed his eyes, too.

He saw starships hidden in lakes on foreign worlds. Alarms

rang in a small village, children lined up, as he experienced the overwhelming fear of the planetary evacuation. Clustered in a tight formation, hinged together, ships of varying sizes orbited a red, cratered moon half consumed in shadow, the ships awaiting yet another escape.

Left behind with a survey team, he hobbled across a ruined planet, his spacesuit's headlamps piercing the murky atmosphere. Bodies emerged from the shadows—frozen in time like sculptures— horns and bony remains raised to the sky, skeletal arms reaching for stars, mouths agape, torsos half-buried in magma, doomed. His people died here, their remains now combined with the surface, their visible limbs now composed of a black, frothy scoria, tinted scarlet in his helmet beams.

What happened to them?

But as soon as the question materialized, he knew the answer: *the boleeron.*

He knew it would happen again and again on many other worlds as his people fled, seeking refuge, forever escaping, forever pursued by that violent race.

They fled world after world.

Then the memories shifted. Since Inlarah, his people had lasted the longest on Earth. Long enough to forget they were ever pursued. But the war. The war. Starships plummeted, bursting, throwing flames onto Australia's sands, forcing new craters deep into the ground. In every country—weapons caches, technology centers, communication networks—all consumed in quick flashes. He saw satellites shattered against the starry night like flicks of streaking spark. The remainder of his people's fleet waged final battles over the seas of Celebes, Timor, Arafura, Coral, and Tasman, defending his people on Australia and New Zealand. During these final days of the Great Earth War, he witnessed the last starships ignite above distant swells, their ancient bodies raining into the sea, sacrificed against an unknown weapon, one hidden even from the *Memoriams'* mental reach.

Most of their precious new home—Earth—lay in ruin, their union with humanity severed.

Then Kene was in a male's body only a little older than himself—inside a younger Palor. He and Loy strode away from the river, the green valley and the towers at their backs. Anthro, the encampment, did not yet exist. The trees and grasses guided their path as they journeyed until the city could no longer be seen. The forest darkened around them, and the sun set behind endless mountains.

They reached four rocks overlooking a dark valley.

Very cautiously, Loy approached the rocks and gestured for his companion to follow. Loy's hand then passed over one of the rocks, and the second rock from the end immediately disappeared into the grass. A hole—all that remained. Loy entered.

Sticking a careful toe below ground, Kene found steps and descended into a dimly lit corridor. Light spread over them, but Kene couldn't identify the source. The tubular hallway's walls, ceiling, and floor self-illuminated. Loy walked far ahead, and Kene rushed to join him.

The passageway opened into a great, cavernous storage room. Inside this domed bay, a large big-bellied starship, the cockpit high in the nose tip, rested like a great celestial whale hibernating in a secret womb.

Kene's gaze traveled the ship's surface, and he remembered the weapons installed over the course of their interstellar exodus. The name, etched into the hull with the fine curves and angles of the Anshahar language, was *Essariah*.

"I've been on this ship before," Kene found himself saying.

"Many times," Loy said.

"This ship is old."

"Ancient."

Kene approached the fuselage and put his hand on the surprisingly clean surface. The ancient ship seemed new, a lifeboat awaiting disaster, a vessel that had survived interstellar space. The only known starship to have remained intact after the Great Earth War.

Humans—and his own people—would raise armies to capture a vessel as rare as this. And Palor was showing him where it hid. As he touched the massive flank, the memory faded.

He opened his eyes.

Palor lowered the *kin* and then wrapped his hand around Kene's neck, resting his forehead against Kene's. Were their scars touching? Kene wasn't sure.

Palor whispered, "You see? You see what I have for you? You're the only one I can give this to." He gently squeezed Kene's neck. "Memory *is* identity. We lose it, and we lose everything."

Kene looked into Palor's eyes.

"I was going to wait to show you. I'm glad I didn't."

Kene, who hadn't touched another person in over a year, instinctively fell forward into Palor's arms. His cheek came to rest on the old one's shoulder.

Palor said, almost inaudibly, "Don't run away again. We have to trust each other."

Their embrace tightened.

"Only launch the ship, only lead others there as a last resort."

K<small>ENE CARRIED OUT A RECONNAISSANCE OF</small> R<small>O'S EVERY MOVE.</small>

He spied on Ro and Deliz standing between the last two habitats near the forest, shaded as they spoke quietly in the mornings. Some nights, before dusk, Deliz and Ro sparred with wooden weapons in a dirt circle. Other times, they used their fists, bare boned hands impacting their rigid flesh. Deliz, towering over her lithe frame, collapsed with a blow to his neck. Again and again, she defeated him with bewildering speed.

Ro often wandered into the forest and climbed a great tree at the thicket's edge. Kene spied on her from the bushes and ferns, watching her dangle in the high branches. She studied Naven endlessly from those trees. Once, he found her in the forest, a small *kin* in her hand, a size he'd never seen before. She squatted over a tiny animal—Kene didn't know its type. The animal had soft, short fur and large black eyes. It was struggling among the leaves. Ro stood abruptly and strolled away, back into the woods. When Kene no longer heard her footfalls, he emerged from his hiding place and cautiously approached the animal.

It had a round nub for a tail and large back feet. Its limbs rotated uncontrollably, pawing at the air as if trying to right itself. He grabbed a nearby stick and helped the animal onto its feet, but it still struggled, unable to coax its limbs to move in unison.

"It's broken."

Kene jumped and spun around.

Ro stood behind him. "You follow me every day."

Kene took a step back.

"So he's warned you about me? And you're afraid? Fear is born from what we don't understand." She moved toward him, her *kin* held out.

"What did you do to it?" Kene continued backing away from her.

"Here, take the other end of my *kin*. Press it to your scar. I'll show you there's nothing to fear from me."

Panic ignited in him, and his senses heightened as fear took over. He turned and ran far into the forest until he hacked and coughed from the chill air. Then he stopped and listened. The *Fugue* hadn't pursued him.

He never told Palor about Ro and the animal. But a few days later, he observed with dismay as Anthro's porters erected a permanent habitat for her.

KENE'S WILL TO ESCAPE, HIS DOUBT IN HIMSELF, DIMINISHED LIKE A fading tide, his apprehension soaking down into the sand. At night, instead of escaping the encampment and running along the river to the beach, he escaped into other people's lives. He confronted the foreign memories pulsing through his mind. He jumped into the unordered array, wading through it and allowing himself to be immersed. Learning to process the memories, he gained new vigor, exhaustion no longer claiming him. And when he'd dug through all the ones he had, reliving his favorite lives, he found that he wanted more. But Palor warned him that bearing a lighter load at first was still the safest course. Too many imprints too fast could damage him, even kill him.

As his new *Memoriam* understanding blossomed, so did his body. Over the next seven years, his horns grew, no longer the budding, fuzzy nubs of his youth. He sought relationships with the others and came to know all Anthro's inhabitants, but the relationships remained formal, the others keeping a respectful distance. Even Elma, the medic and his tutor in human languages, cast her eyes down when Kene asked her to play a game or take a walk, her response always: "I can't."

Palor grew old, his skin shriveling tight around his facial bones and emphasizing the ridge of his forehead that hadn't been there years earlier. His eyelids drooped at times, and Kene often found him staring at the habitat's plastic wall, lost in thought and unaware of Kene's presence, until Kene softly touched his shoulder, the tap coaxing him back from reverie.

What favorite memories were you exploring, old one? Kene never asked, sensing that his travels through the *remembrance* were as private as his own.

Over the years, his people travelled from as far as Lakarta's northernmost tip and Australia's Victoria, arriving randomly in Anthro, seeking council with Palor. Others, sick and dying, elderly and frail, arrived too, sometimes in droves, hiking single file on the river trail, and Palor would place the *kin* between their horns, making their lives his own. Messengers arrived from the leadership council and envoys from the parliament as well as visiting commanders. He saw them all.

Marcus, the human messenger, aged too, retiring his duties to his daughter, Alta, now a young woman. Kene liked to watch for her with his back propped against the steep hill, looking over the valley for a reddish brown dot against the green. She blasted from Naven's gates, her craft shooting across the fields, flattening swaths of meadow, the long grass blades whipping in her wake. He marveled at the craft, once mass-produced, now one of a kind. Two large air fans spinning and adjusting made up almost its entirety— giant engines with a seat placed on top. The craft sheathed her legs in tight troughs that gripped her muscles, sensing every pull or push and adjusting accordingly. She leaned forward, her arms forming a partial circle in front of her, forearms resting inside sleeves upheld by flexible supports. She flew over the river, the fans jettisoning water into the air, sometimes creating small, fleeting rainbows.

After parking her craft just outside Anthro, Alta would stroll through the encampment with tense muscles, as if bracing her body against some impending hurt. She rarely took her mask off. The blue veins in her arms and neck pulsed under her skin's unique transparency. Short stubble covered her hornless skull, never allowed to grow longer than a fingernail. She distanced herself from these others—these aliens—moving away if any came near.

Kene spoke to her sometimes: "How is your day?" "Yours is lovely." "Your journey are well to here?"—practicing his English. She never responded, but one time smiled, before treading away, her skinny frame stiffly upright as her hip bones swayed from side to side. He cursed himself for losing the token she gave him all those years before, wishing he still had it to show her, to remind her of her kindness. Before sleep overtook him, Alta drifted into his imagination along with the idea, the impossible coincidence— or destiny, he didn't know which—of arriving on a planet with a species so genetically close to his own. A species they could reproduce with. The mystery inspired awe in him.

A LOUD NOISE BROKE KENE'S CONCENTRATION, AND HIS EYES BLINKED open. Above, a light breeze blew the forest's leaves. Earlier, he had hiked to his usual spot near the small pond, a place where he processed the morning's imprint. The noise sounded like a blast, an explosion echoing in the distance. He stood, listening. But no more explosions came. He thought he could hear yelling but wasn't sure. He tensed, his body instinctively bracing.

He raced through the woods, between the trees, and hopped over rocks and felled trunks. As he got closer to Anthro, a metallic aroma entered his nostrils. People cried out and screamed. He saw villagers dashing between the habitats as smoke rose, a yellow haze in the air.

"Kene!" Someone called.

He sprinted up the slope. Smoke climbed the air in puffs from the encampment's center. As he neared, he discovered it was Palor's habitat. A crowd gathered around a body on the ground.

"Palor!" Kene pushed through the onlookers. Palor lay there, his skin bloodied, his eyes closed, and Ro leaned over him with a *kin* connected to both their scars. She opened her eyes, tried to stand, but then collapsed next to Palor.

She's taken the remembrance. The idea stunned him, and, for a moment, he felt as if in a dream, his limbs immobile, frozen with shock. *If she dies, we lose everything.*

Deliz dropped down beside her. "The messenger. The human female was the last person with him." Deliz felt for Ro's pulse. "The habitat exploded, and we dragged Palor out. He was still alive. Ro acted when you did not respond. She said this would be the only chance."

Kene wrenched himself out of his shock and then knelt, feeling Palor's veins for life. "He's dead." *Was the imprint complete?* Kene met Ro's exhausted gaze. "Ro has to rest."

Deliz picked her up and carried her away.

A deep burn ravaged Kene's insides. Blasts and acrid aromas from explosions—memories not his own—swirled with his senses. A welling of images and emotions shook within him, wanting to take over his consciousness and place him in a *Memoriam* trance. But he resisted the flood of memory.

Anthro's inhabitants stood around him. Palor's head rested in his hands, burn wounds slashed across his face.

"What now?" Kene whispered to Palor. "I'm not ready."

Kene found himself squeezing Palor's hands, searching again, even though he knew he'd find no life there. As he held onto his mentor, a memory forced its way into his consciousness. An old memory. A short child, crying as her mother placed her in the cryotube. The tube's hatch closed, and it was dark. Then effervescent lights shone through the glass peepholes and landed on her pearly skin. Slowly the chamber's atmosphere altered, providing a warm thickness for her to breathe, and her eyes fluttered to the rhythm of her heart. When she awoke, her mother and everyone she knew would be long dead. She would have to let go.

Kene opened his eyes and slowly released the old man's hands.

He stepped over the body and into the smoldering habitat. The floor burned his feet, but he barely noticed, grief dampening the pain to a numb throb. He brushed away ashes on the floor and smoking pieces of satchel to uncover Palor's *kin*, glowing multicolored with heat. Wrapping his hand in his robe, he picked it up, warmth searing through the cloth. He held it hidden in a fold of his robe as he stepped back outside.

Could Alta do something like this? He didn't want to accept it.

Now it was up to him to preserve peace with the humans.

"Find Alta," Kene said to the gathered crowd. "But don't hurt her. We'll deliver her to Naven."

IN THE MORNING, AFTER CLEANSING HIS FACE WITH SOME WATER, Kene found a tiny child waiting outside his habitat.

"Ro's awake," she announced and led Kene to where she rested in Elma's care.

"She's still weak," Elma patted Ro's arm, "but conscious."

Kene pulled a stool over to the bedside. "How are you feeling?"

Ro gazed up at him with a smug expression. His was a dangerous position. Not only did Ro know everything about Palor and have all the memories, but she knew everything Palor thought about Kene, all his plans for Kene. He had no idea where she stood, what she would do.

"I'm better." Ro turned her gaze to the ceiling. "But how are you?"

Kene didn't know what she meant. "In shock."

"My mentor died long before my training was complete. It can change you, but you have to be strong and practice your gifts, and you'll eventually master them, learning to control your memories."

Kene stared at her.

"Your apprenticeship is over."

A hot spark of fright overtook his body. "Imprint the *remembrance* on me."

"No. It would kill you. You're not ready." Ro closed her eyes. "I will find my own disciple. You may be a candidate for *remembrance,* but you know nothing of forgetting." She smiled as if at a private joke and then opened her eyes and slowly turned toward him. "Tonight, you'll finally be leaving Anthro. You always wanted to leave. Didn't you?"

"Not since I was a child."

"You still are a child." Seriousness overtook Ro's expression. "I'm now the *Memoriam.*"

"You've had no training."

"I've had plenty."

"And Alta?"

"Alta killed Palor with some device. I can see the memory clearly." She gestured to a slate on her desk. Kene picked it up. A message from Naven expressed regret at Palor's murder. In it, a decree granting permission to prosecute any human involved in a hope to show goodwill at the advent of peace. It also recognized Ro as the new *Memoriam*.

He gazed up from the message. "What did you tell them?"

Ro glanced away. "Alta will be executed."

Kene returned to his habitat and splashed his face with more cold water from the washing bowl, rinsing again as if to cleanse his thoughts, wash away his grief. Outside, everyone hurried to and fro, packing up supplies and dismantling their homes.

What had she done? He peeked his head out and touched a passing child's shoulder. "What's happening?"

The child cast her eyes to the dirt. "We've been disbanded."

"All of you?"

The child nodded, and Kene waved her away.

Was this all he'd earned? A *Fugue*'s disregard? There must be a way to protest, to fight back and retrieve what was rightfully his.

In the afternoon, black figures appeared on the river trail. And soon twenty *Parhata* entered Anthro. Kene stood with the other onlookers as the soldiers passed them without acknowledgement. The *Parhata* marched straight to Deliz, who stood, arms crossed, at the town's center.

After watching the new soldiers situate themselves, Kene returned to his habitat to think. Could they mount a resistance? Would Palor agree? Was it worth the risk of life?

But whatever the dangers, his mind always returned to the truth. Ro hadn't been chosen. She was a *Memoriam* by circumstance. What right did she have to take away the *remembrance?* She hadn't even completed her own training all those years ago.

The Essariah. He lay back and stared at the ceiling, trying to suppress his fright. Had she delved that deeply into the memories yet? Did she know the ship's hiding place? Did she plan to start a war with Naven, one they could finally win with that vessel?

Throughout the afternoon, the people of Anthro stopped by his tent with food parcels, gifts, and well-wishes. He hugged them all. "Find us when you're back in Lakarta," many of them said. Tent flap pulled back, he watched as the biggest group hiked single-file over the river trail, leaving the valley.

That night, Deliz came to his habitat. "Time to leave."

"You know the council won't allow this." Kene rolled his bedclothes so he could carry the bundle on his back.

Deliz only stared at him.

"Why are you helping her?"

"She's the new *Memoriam.* I'm sworn to protect her. The sooner you accept this, the sooner you'll understand my actions. You're no longer an apprentice. You're not needed here."

"Where do I go?"

"Go home."

"And these soldiers?"

"Whatever Palor told you, you're not in charge anymore."

"You've sworn to protect the *Memoriam and* his disciple—"

"Enough." Deliz stepped forward quickly. He towered over Kene. "Get up."

Outside, three *Parhata* pushed Alta's hovercraft toward the forest. Kene chuckled, despite his sorrow. The craft housed ancient technology, yet too advanced for these soldiers to figure out. Perhaps the craft allowed only Alta to ride it.

Kene strolled toward the ocean. Deliz followed him at a distance. How long would Deliz follow? Kene continued his hike, the sun setting before he reached the beach. When he finally turned, the trail behind him was empty.

The *Essariah* flashed again into his mind. Ro would soon remember it if she hadn't already. But if he secured the vessel first, how long could he keep it from her? He certainly did not know how to launch it. Without the complete *remembrance* as his guide, he could not expect to prevail. And if he secured the ship first, he might miss this chance to save the *remembrance* while Ro was still weak.

Kene sprinted up the side of the hill, steep with rocks and unseen obstacles now that night had descended. He tripped, regained his footing, and then fell again. The sea air at his back, he stumbled farther up, high above the trail and river. He stepped cautiously through the brush on the slope, feeling his way toward the ridge. His knees and shins throbbed with cuts, and his ankles tightened with soreness. He could no longer see the trail below. The river's rushing, its water flowing over rocks, concealed him.

After an hour or so, a fire glow shimmered over the weeds as the final downslope lay ahead. There was only the steep descent between him and Anthro. He reclined on the hill, well out of the light, and observed dark figures pass to and fro in front of the fires. Only eight habitats remained, including two at the base of the hill, one each for Deliz, Elma, and Ro, and a large one for the twenty *Parhata*. Strangely enough, his former home had not been removed. He shivered, not so much from the cold, but from his resolution to go back down there.

What was he thinking? He imagined having to fight the *Parhata*. Trained fighters, professional soldiers. But then, what else could he do? Let his species forget? Let Ro destroy the *remembrance* and the peace with Naven? This was the hardest part. Waiting. The doubts.

He stopped shuddering and focused on the hill's base and the quieting camp.

He waited.

Anthro's firelights flickered out, one by one. As he stretched out his legs, he once more traced the perimeter of the town with his gaze, watching for movement. He descended, slowly and quietly, the wind and river still masking his movements. He stopped, and then he saw a figure moving between the tents. Kene lay in the grass, well out of sight. The figure passed him without stopping.

Deliz? He didn't wait for anyone else. He darted behind what used to be Gol's home, using the tent's bulk to conceal himself.

He stepped very quietly, heading toward his former habitat. Faint, muffled crying emanated from inside. He crouched low and entered through the plastic flaps. Too dark to see. He searched around the floor, his hand fitting over a head, a human face, soft stubble on a hornless skull.

"Alta."

She stopped squirming.

He pulled the blindfold from her eyes. "Don't scream." He removed the gag from her mouth.

Alta coughed and spit.

Kene felt around for his water flute and poured the liquid into her mouth.

"Thank you."

He touched her face with his hand.

"I didn't do it. You have to believe me. Whatever they tell you." She coughed. "We need the peace."

He wanted to believe her. Even without proof, he wanted to believe her.

"I'll return for you." He lifted the blindfold back up to her face.

"No. What are you doing?"

"Just in case they peek in here. Now lie down. It's only for a little while. I'll be back soon."

Alta nodded, biting her lip as Kene replaced the muzzle and tied it around her head. "Lie back now." He guided her to the floor.

Outside, he saw no one. Stepping through the tent flaps, he made his way toward Ro's home. Many of the old habitats lay broken down and packed in piles. He cautiously stepped over them, Ro's habitat just ahead. A yellow glow brightened its plastic walls. Was she still awake?

Crouching low, he approached, close enough to peek under the entry flaps. Candlelight flickered inside. Ro's limbs sprawled across the bed, resting. She faced away from the entrance. The slate from Naven still lay on her desk.

He withdrew his *kin* as low voices trickled in from behind.

There wouldn't be another chance.

Ro rolled over and blinked, opening her eyes. Kene vaulted toward her as her lips parted. But he covered her mouth with his hand and forced her head back, placing the *kin* on her scar. Her arms and legs flailed, but, still weak from the imprint, she could do no more than paw at him. She forced her eyes open with a willpower that sent chills through him, her lids quivering with strain. He needed them closed. He brought his mouth close to her face, and, in one quick burst, blew air over her eyes.

She blinked.

His hand shot from her mouth to her lids, keeping them shut. He pressed his scar against the *kin* as she let out a half-yelp, her breath briefly hitting his face.

He closed his eyes.

KENE STUMBLED ACROSS ANTHRO'S EMPTY HOME PLOTS, DIZZY, THE *kin* in one hand and the messenger slate in the other. Memories welled up within him like bloated bodies drifting downriver, bobbing and rolling against rocks and currents—their dreams, hopes, and failures flooding his veins, shaking every nerve, increasing his pulse until his skin vibrated. The swollen river could not be dammed, and soon he could not bear the noise. Hands covering his ears, memories rushed freely, uncontrolled, drowning his senses.

He tried to direct his path toward the tree line but collapsed. He crawled back to his own habitat, where Alta waited. Sick and weak, he pulled himself inside. Shivering against the habitat's thin walls, he tried to focus on his own memories, the ones made when he first arrived here, but every time he grasped one, some foreign memory ripped through by association. Palor's early memories filled Kene's consciousness, and he saw Loy across a table, a small lamp casting his features in blue light. "*Memoriams* aren't born; they're created. That is the final secret I have for you."

His muscles shook with fierce spasms. *Imprinting the* remembrance *was a mistake.* He shouldn't have tampered, shouldn't have taken so much. Smells he did not recognize, sounds that he knew were not there overlaid his vision. The habitat melted, forming spirals, pulling him under like a whirlpool. His head throbbed, but when he closed his eyes, he was immersed in faces, worlds, lives not his own.

No escape.

Palor's thoughts surfaced: *He started too old. He will take it too hard.* Then a thousand voices echoed in his skull. Kene grabbed his head, the voices clamoring for volume, all the memories from his predecessors invading. And then hiding beneath his hallucinations, for a brief moment, he discovered his own voice: *You did not pass a test—you survived a procedure.*

The forty children's names who had never come back from that final test...

"We're the only two," Palor's voice whispered.

Because no other child had lived.

Schematics, equations, and plans proliferated a flat surface. He was in front of a desk, in a female's body. She constructed a small device—an explosive—then, with Elma's help, coiled an old tunic around the small, round object. The memory shifted to another: while watching Naven's gates open, she slid down a tree and rushed back into the encampment. She handed a small, cotton-wrapped package to Deliz.

Deliz nodded and soon left, heading for Palor's tent.

The blast pierced his ears, but did not shake the ground.

Kene opened his eyes. He still lay on the dirt floor, the space around him twisting and melting into rainbow streams of fading color overlaying the darkness. His heart pounded, screaming to break free. His fingers dug into his chest, unable to penetrate muscle and bone. The pressure. His body jolted as if being crushed under the flood-weight of memory.

Ro and Deliz killed Palor.

Alta's muffled whispers came from somewhere to his side.

His eyes. He could not hold them open.

His lids fell shut.

Ro's despair bubbled in him, her hurt unraveling before him like a dying beast, its organs and insides laid bare. Special. Chosen. She believed this more than he had—still believed it—for she was not created but something different...an anomaly.

A *Fugue.*

In Lakarta, she travelled outside the cities, sleeping in valleys carved by fallen starships. She trained herself among the half-buried vessels peeking from their tombs. Derelict, molested by dirt and weeds, overhangs created by cockpits or engine casings kept her dry. She battled her fear and sorrow. She mastered the memories Loy had given her, the worst of the worst. She learned to control the power to forget and suppress. She could choose. She could determine a course for her people that wasn't hampered by the past, by the knowledge of what *had been.* Her ability to forget their history, their pain, their staunch ethics, would give them freedom to make different choices. The right choices. She could edit the *remembrance,* passing on only what was useful for progress.

The day she joined the *Parhata* swelled in him. Then the memory of an elegant figure standing on a balcony.

The commander of the North, Valnia Alteiri, her jewelry lightly chiming, leaned in to whisper, "We need a strong *Memoriam.*"

Ro bowed, kneeling before Alteiri.

"Naven will collapse in time if left alone." Alteiri held Ro's shoulders, her lavender eyes somber, her face strong and exquisite. "You will make a fine *Memoriam.*"

Kene opened his eyes again, the space around him now indiscernible, wrapped in some horrid unreality, his senses merging in confusion. He smelled the sounds of footsteps from centuries past and could hear the thump of starlight streaming in through the entry flap's slits. Pain exploded through him. His spine heaved with a fierce spasm, arching his torso upward, his muscles screaming, begging for him to let go.

The tent spun like a vortex.

He struggled to inhale, but choked as if on his own throat flesh.

I'm dying.

And when he felt his body drained of its will, its strength, a face emerged from the spinning tent. A young bright face, one that could only belong to Palor. "You're ready." Then he saw thousands of *Memoriams* standing like lit beacons in a thick, confused magma. Their lives injected meaning into the total of the past. Hope kindled within him. Perhaps, with their help, he could process the enormous imprint.

Pink light seeped through slits in the plastic. Kene's lids blinked, struggling to open. His head throbbed, his body sore all over as if he had been beaten.

What happened?

As he gained strength, he slowly recalled Palor's young face, the words "You're ready" still echoing in his head.

Alta murmured next to him.

Kene lifted the blindfold from her face and removed the gag.

She jumped when she saw him. "I thought you were dead. I thought someone would hear you. You sounded in so much pain." She stared up at him as he untied her.

"I have a place to hide, up in the mountains, in the wilderness."

"Take me back to Naven." Her voice cracked.

"They'll kill us."

"Why?"

Kene shuffled the materials on the ground, looking for the message. He found the slate covered in dirt and handed it to her. "They agreed to your execution."

She studied the words, tears forming in her eyes. Then she let the slate tumble to the ground. "You trust me?"

"You're innocent."

"You trust me? A human? From Naven?"

He gazed at her worn face, recalling their brief childhood together, remembering her hair draped at odd angles, her smile. "Come. We have to hurry." He pushed her through first, then followed. They ran from Anthro, racing along the base of the hill.

"Kene!" a voice called from behind.

He glimpsed the medic, Elma, standing between two habitats, a witness to their escape.

"What have you done to her?" Elma cried.

Kene and Alta dashed past the last tents and raced down the slope to her hovercraft at the field's edge. She reached the vehicle first and straddled the seat, slipping her legs into the troughs and her arms into the sleeves, the craft tightening around her muscles. She pushed her legs down and the fans hummed to life. Kene jumped on behind her. She lunged forward with her arms, and the craft launched.

"Hold on." Alta kicked back, stretching her body. The craft responded by accelerating and lengthening its own body in imitation.

She curved the craft's trajectory. "Where are we going?" she yelled.

"Through the forest, up the trail."

They wove between trees, the sun flickering through the canopy and low-hanging branches. Kene held on to Alta, telling her the way. They accelerated under a stony mountaintop and then glided down to its base, where a little stream bordered the slopes and trickled over rocks. The hovercraft kicked up a fan of water as they passed.

Soon they arrived at four rocks on a grassy knoll.

"Here." Kene slid off as Alta slowed the craft.

He waved his hand over the rock like Loy had in the memory, hoping this was going to work. Nothing happened. Kene looked around the knoll for other rock formations, panic filling his head. But then the rock sank into the ground. He laughed and gripped Alta's hand and led her down into the passageway. The entry closed behind them and a long corridor self-illuminated—a tunnel of curved light panels.

"What is this?" Alta's voice echoed in the strange hall.

"You'll see."

When they exited the tunnel into the storage bay, Kene, too tired for awe, watched Alta's frame tense, her head tilting upward, as she stared in wonder at what lay before them. "That takes up the whole mountain." She whispered.

The curved fuselage occupied almost the entire bay, displaying no sharp angles or edges, like a giant porpoise's rounded form. Blackened half-moon windows dappled its pearly skin in seemingly random arrangements, as the bay's ceiling lights created shimmering reflections on the vessel's surface.

"Your people kept this?"

He swallowed and then nodded. "A lifeboat."

"They lied." Alta shook her head. "They said they'd trade all their technology to stay on Earth."

"We kept some...it was a long time ago." Kene opened one of the hatches. "There are rooms inside. And food."

In an oblong lift, they traveled up the many levels to the top deck, where he directed her to the commander's room. "I'll take the cabin just below."

Alta grabbed his shoulder before he could leave. "Will they follow us here?"

"Yes. We don't have much time. Maybe a night to rest." Kene hesitated for a moment. "She knows everything I know about this place and this vessel. I can't stop her from finding it. I can't prevent her from entering."

"So what do we do?"

Kene's eyes closed. He couldn't answer her now. His limbs pulled him down with fatigue, the weight of processing the *remembrance* still bearing on him.

Alta took his arm and walked him to his cabin.

They bathed separately. Then Alta rejoined him, and they ate preserved foods. Kene's body shook with chills when he finally lay down. His brow was moist and feverish. Alta soaked a cloth and wiped away the sweat. She stayed with him during the night, falling asleep next to him on the suspended bed.

In the morning, Alta seemed deep in thought. "You can't fly this can you?"

"No."

"With all your memories, you still can't do it."

"I remember how. But I don't have the practice. I don't have the reflexes. The memories don't give me skills and abilities, only the information and the sensation of the experience." He turned his head toward her. "But I'll show you how."

"Me?"

"Yes."

"I can't fly this. I have no idea how."

Kene turned away from her. "You can fly it. You have to. Or we'll soon be dead and so will Naven."

That afternoon, Kene, feeling better, sat outside on one of the rocks marking the hanger's entrance. He breathed in the fresh air and bathed his face in the sun's warmth. Gazing out over the mountains, he noticed movement. Kene jolted upright. A thin black line of figures marched up the slope, followed by wheeled vehicles. Dread rattled through his body, vanquishing his prior sense of healing.

The *Fugue* had brought an army.

He rushed back into the hanger and hobbled, still weak, to the *Essariah*. He found Alta inside her cabin.

"They're coming for us," Kene said.

"What now?"

"We launch."

"I told you. I can't fly this thing."

"You don't have a choice."

Kene led her to the cockpit and showed her the pilot's seat. Long tentacle-like vines curled around the seat, hooking into the air above its inside back.

He gestured for her to sit.

"I don't know how to fly this. I don't even know what these are."

"Wait a moment."

A circular panel rose from the floor, and Kene slid his fingers through the air above it. The pilot's seat morphed like clay sculpted by invisible hands. Troughs formed for her legs, reminiscent of those on her hovercraft. She placed her legs inside and the material tightened around them, revealing her muscles. Forearm sleeves rose from the floor in front of the seat and adjusted themselves to Alta's position as the hooked vines disappeared into the seat's base.

"Something you're more used to?"

Alta grinned.

"You pilot it the same way, with your body. The panels in front of you indicate pitch, roll, yaw, and your surroundings, just like on your craft." Kene turned away from her and moved his fingers over another panel. "I'll open the hanger's dome. Get ready to launch us."

"No." Alta lifted her legs, and the troughs released them.

She stepped down from the pilot's seat.

"What are you doing? We don't have time."

"Not before you promise me something."

Kene flicked his fingers over the panel, and the hangar's dome cracked open, an expanding crescent of brilliant sun flooding the bay. The light entered the cockpit through the large bubble window in front of them.

Alta stepped closer to him. "Palor's work. It wasn't just for peace. He was saving us. Our defenses, our weapons, they don't work anymore. We're bluffing." Her eyes teared. "We have no more materials. No more iron and rubber. If I help you save this ship, someday, when the time comes, you must help me save Naven."

Kene stared at her for a moment, thinking of Palor. The memories around Naven were varied and complex. He could not sort through them now. But if he still believed Naven was the key to peace. "You trust me? An inlari? An alien?" He smiled. "I will help."

Alta jumped back into the troughs, which again tightened around her legs. She kicked down and the *Essariah* shook with ignition. The ship ascended, passing between the bay doors above. Kene strapped himself into the nearest seat as the cockpit hummed with increasing vibration. When the vessel cleared the underground hanger, Alta leaned to her side and pushed her arms forward, navigating the ship around in a forty-five degree turn. Then she punched with her fists, and they blasted away from the mountain. As they accelerated, the bubble window shifted, narrowing to a point. The cockpit changed too, the walls and ceiling bending inward. Panels disappeared and lights dimmed. Kene's seat slid closer to Alta's.

She pushed down with her feet and pulled her arms back to her chest, the pilot seat molding to her extended form. The ship lurched upward, sky and clouds filling the window.

"What are you doing?" Kene yelled above the ship's screeches and rumbles.

"Ever wonder what Earth looks like from space?"

The force increased against his body, pressing him back into his seat. The pressure rippled over his skin as he dug his fingers into the cushion. Pulsing tremors throbbed through him until they occurred so quickly they became one force, one singular sensation.

The vessel shot upward, forcing its way through the atmosphere, cutting through clouds and the planet's upper hemispheres. The blue sky dissolved to black, and millions of stars greeted them as the *Essariah* trembled, rocketing them away from Earth, away from Naven, away from humans and inlaris.

Then the pressure released his body, and the tremors ceased.

Alta extended one arm forward while pulling back with the other, and the ship swung around. The window before them filled with navy seas and swirling clouds, a stark shadow basking the surface on the left. Earth did not look decimated from here, did not look radiated or vaporized, only still and tranquil, apart from time, like a memory.

UNDERGROUND INTELLIGENCE

ELAINE CHAO

108 YEARS AFC

SHE SAT ALONE in the predawn light, sheltered by the large rock formation. This was her safe spot, exposed as it was to the rest of the manicured slave park in the eastern part of Wellington. It faced the ocean, and even though Ān-tíng couldn't hear the waves from where she was, she could at least see the gray-green waters of the Pacific Ocean.

"Hey." Nate's husky baritone rumbled quietly, soft in the morning stillness. This was their ritual. Almost every morning, she navigated through the dark warren of underground tunnels that riddled the underside of the city like the roots of a large tree. When she neared the park, she slipped on a white tunic and clipped the deactivated slave collar around her neck, then stepped out from the large drain and into the pre-dawn light. Even this early, she was far from the first human abroad, as slaves headed to early morning work shifts in households across the city. Ān-tíng then clambered up the steps on the back side of the rock and worked her way to the eastern face, where a small indentation—more a shallow cavern than a ledge—allowed her some shelter from the elements.

Nate handed her a mug and poured his beverage of choice from the thermos he had filled at headquarters. The rich, sharp smell of coffee overwhelmed her senses for a moment, and she accepted it without comment, even though her own preference for these tête-à-têtes was hot chocolate.

"Thanks," she acknowledged. Their morning ritual had taken on a comfortable cadence after so many years. At first, he had followed her as a love-addled adolescent newly recruited for the Ànchù, all scrawny arms and legs, his narrow nose and startling blue-green eyes dominating a thin face. And after months of telling him that a woman eight years his senior wasn't interested in a boy of sixteen, they had settled into a friendship that was as warm and comfortable as a winter blanket.

They sat in silence, watching the sky get brighter as the minutes passed by.

"You ever wonder what it would be like to live at peace?" Nate asked, his voice velvety soft.

"We're at war," Ān-tíng reminded him, taking a sip of the coffee to hide her irritation. It was bitter and dark, the way that Nate preferred. She had gotten used to it.

"The Great War was long before our lifetimes, Ting." He almost managed the accent on her name correctly, but she had forgiven him that slight years ago.

"Despite what they're still doing to our people?" she replied resentfully. "And, I might add, what they did to our families."

She knew it was a low blow to bring up their families. Everyone in the Ànchù had similar stories: their slave families had smuggled them out at birth to safety. These children, the few that survived, were raised by the Ànchù to understand the inlaris as no one else could. From birth, they had watched hours upon hours of inlari media on a daily basis, learning to speak the inlari language, Anshahar, as natives. Many, like she and Nate, often spoke Anshaglish—a natural mixture of Anshahar and English.

Ān-tíng had been one of the lucky ones; her family had been local, their inlari master absent for days, sometimes weeks, at a time. Her parents and grandparents had visited frequently, speaking to her in the dying Mandarin language as often as they could. She knew just enough to hold conversations with her family, but her thoughts, more often than not, sang out in Anshahar. The inlaris had a certain symmetry to their music and language, something she could viscerally understand, even more than the tones of the driving bhangra or flamenco or the ambient trance that floated through the lab whenever someone had their speakers blaring.

Inlari music comforted her, offering her a solace that she couldn't quite verbalize. She had learned to describe the different musical styles that played in inlari homes and shops, from the driving, insistent polyrhythms of the classic dances to the more floating modern pieces that reflected the long inlari exodus from their homeworld to Ān-tíng's. To Earth.

Nate's voice was silken, placating. "I know what they've done, Ting. I just wonder sometimes what it might be like to live at peace instead of war."

"There is no peace while there are human slaves, Nate. No

matter how much they wanted it to be a good thing, our people are suffering underneath slavery." Ān-tíng narrowed her eyes. It was an old debate between the two of them, one that only served to remind her that Nate was *not* the type of man for her. "Besides, we're *hēi-kè*. According to the inlaris, we're somewhere between spies and terrorists. They would never accept us as equals." The next sip of coffee seemed even more bitter.

"I can't help but hope."

"Then you're a fool."

He sighed, looking at her from the corner of his eye, as his mouth twisted in reluctant acceptance of her pronouncement. Ān-tíng suspected he still harbored feelings for her, much to the chagrin of some of the younger ladies in the Ànchù. If she could trust what she overheard in the women's locker room, Nate had broken more than his share of hearts. She had to admit that he had turned out nicely, his scrawny frame filling out into a leanly muscled warrior. His face had filled out a little as well, changing from boy to man over the past five years, his jawline now showing more a perpetual five o'clock shadow than juvenile fuzz.

He interrupted the silence. "The winds are changing, you know. I can feel it."

Ān-tíng finished the last of her coffee. "You know I don't believe in that stuff."

"I heard rumors there's a big op being planned. Might be announced today."

"I hope I get to go." Ān-tíng knew she was at the top of her game, one of the primary *hēi-kè*. She, like many of the other *hēi-kè*, was well-versed in inlari technology and could make her way through the typical security system in minutes. Of course, the Ànchù had many different types of specialists, some in combat, some in infiltration, and others in information gathering. But the *hēi-kè* were the most coveted of the lot, as they both deconstructed technologies and reconstructed them for both the Ànchù and the greater Resistance.

"I hope you don't."

She glanced over at Nate's face. His eyebrows furrowed together in fierce concern, and it touched her heart. "You're a good friend, Nate."

He squeezed her hand and leaned against her, shoulder to shoulder, both of them staring toward where the sun barely peeked over the horizon, the streaky clouds overhead turning orange and pink. She felt his solidity through her slave robe and leaned right back into him, resting her head briefly on his shoulder. He really was a dear friend.

"Come on," he said. "It's almost time to report."

"It's time."

Yéh's voice resonated through the Bunker's common room, which was large enough to double as the gym for the sixty-odd members of the Ànchù. They stood in formation at parade rest, each of them wearing the form-fitting black uniforms and subtle insignia of their secret military branch. His flat statement, steely with determination, had permeated the near-silence.

"Today, we initiate the next phase of our plan to liberate humans from the inlari occupation. *This* is the moment we have been working toward: our resources and knowledge of inlari technology and culture have been invaluable in leading us to this mission."

Yéh was a grizzled veteran in his late forties with salt-and-pepper hair cropped close and a burly frame proclaiming his background as a hand-to-hand combat expert. He was not the first Yéh in the Ànchù's history; the titles of Yéh and Nái had passed from the original elderly couple that had, in a prescient moment, built the underground bunker in Wellington as a human refuge in the case of a war with the inlaris. During the Great War, they had wisely kept a veritable village carefully hidden, passed the titles of "grandparents" to two young leaders, and retired to the relative safety of Australia.

Yéh's kind brown eyes scanned the formation of his warriors, the motley crew of teenagers and young adults that comprised the Ànchù. Ān-tíng had learned from the history books that humans had historically been divided among racial and religious lines. It struck her as bizarre that anything as minor as different skin tone would divide a people, but since the Great War, the humans that were once divided against themselves had instead joined against one common enemy: the inlaris. They, from the darkest to the palest, had intermixed in the generations following the Great War, until many didn't even know their own racial makeup. They were simply humans.

Ān-tíng stood next to Nate in formation, a feeling of satisfaction creeping over her. Finally, there would be justice served, and the Ànchù was going to strike once more against the inlaris. Perhaps it would remind the inlaris that humans weren't domesticated beasts.

"As all of you know, General Adam Holden has been in captivity for the past twenty years, serving time for leading the slave revolt in his youth. Our mission today is to liberate him from the grips of the inlaris. *His* freedom is *our* freedom."

A tendril of fear and excitement spiraled through Ān-tíng. Never, even in her wildest dreams, did she think that the Ànchù would be audacious enough to attempt a rescue of General Holden. During her fifteen-year tenure with the organization, Ān-tíng had seen him repeatedly in the inlari news feeds she filtered for information. He had been in his mid-thirties when she first noted his appearance, his hair dark and his frame still robust after five years in captivity. In the intervening years, he had slowly become more frail, moving as if he were arthritic far before his time, the gray spreading from his temples across his scalp, as if the man himself were fading away.

But he was a symbol, and Valnia Altieri, *Madeer* of Lakarta, wanted nothing more than the greatest symbol of human freedom locked in chains, trotted out like an exotic pet every time the inlaris wanted to celebrate their complete dominion over the humans in New Zealand.

For a long moment, the Ànchù breathed as one organism, wrapping their minds around the enormity of their task. To break Holden out of his cell was beyond reckless.

"Half of you will be going on this mission," Yéh said in the stillness. "Half of you will be risking your lives for the future of the human world, while the other half will be continuing our work in case of failure. Those of you who are left behind are just as important as those who go, for if this mission fails, you will be the seed from which the Ànchù grows."

Ān-tíng counted under her breath as name after name was called. Nate's name was called early. After counting past thirty, Ān-tíng had to admit that she had been left out.

"Check in with your commanders for your squad assignments." Yéh paused, gazing over them all with a look of pained compassion. "Dismissed."

Ān-tíng turned to talk to Nate, but he had already walked away to the small crowd of people around the two team commanders that had been named to the Holden mission. When she finally caught his eye, he looked profoundly thankful that she hadn't been recruited.

Hours later, she stood with a lump in her throat as her teammates suited up for an excursion that could very well end their lives. They all understood the risk and had accepted it as a part of their service to the Ànchù. Sacrifice was the norm, and Holden was important enough to risk half of their forces.

And there was Nate, towering over his teammates by half a head, joking with those around him with that easy, goofy smile. But when he saw Ān-tíng, the smile vanished, revealing a tension in his careworn face. She suddenly realized that somehow, they were all older than their years. Despite the constancy of his rapid-fire jokes and laughter, Nate had matured, his soul deepened with years of losing teammates on missions and the strain that human slavery had impressed upon them all. He was no longer the little kid, but was instead fully an adult. The revelation stunned her.

Nate strode across the large room, people side-stepping as he passed by. "Hey," he murmured, crushing her in a hug. "I'm sorry you didn't get on the team. But I'm glad you're not going, because I'd be worried about you."

"You, worried about me?" she repeated, laughing half-heartedly. "You know this entire mission makes me worried about you, right?"

"Aw, Ting, I didn't know you cared." The soft, teasing tone took the sting out of the rebuke. But then his lips were on hers, and she melted into the sensation of being kissed tenderly by someone who wanted her. And for a brief moment, she wanted him, too, in a way that both frightened and thrilled her. But then she pushed away, stepped back, and glared at him. Nate's eyes crinkled at the corners as he grinned at her in his characteristic, lazy way.

He caught her hand in his and squeezed, his thumb caressing her knuckles as he let go. "Don't be mad at me, Ting. I'm a dead man walking."

And then he was gone.

AT NIGHTFALL, ĀN-TÍNG FOUND HERSELF HUDDLED IN THE BOX hedge, facing a small, human-style house. As the crow flew, the house was a mere kilometer and a half from where she had witnessed the sun crest over the water line of Weka Bay. From this location, she could practically hear the water lapping against the protected shoreline.

Stiff breezes carried the tang of the bay well inland, bringing with it the chill of the Pacific Ocean. Ān-tíng shivered in the hedge but trusted that her black suit would keep her heat signature hidden and help her remain undiscovered in the shadows.

It struck her as profoundly unfair that while thirty of her teammates, Nate included, were beginning their assault against the detention center, Ān-tíng had been sent on a simple *retrieval* mission, stealing a prototype of what was supposed to be some kind of ansible from an elderly inlari researcher. And while the promise of instantaneous communication was tantalizing, it still didn't compare to both the risk and the glory of breaking General Holden out of his cell.

Ān-tíng could tell someone was in the house—one person, moving slowly, turned lights on and off as he passed from kitchen to dining room to living room. She waited patiently, leaning into the hedge for warmth, until all of the lights were out. She waited another hour before shaking out her legs and gliding through the moonlight to the back of the house.

The lock was an old-style mechanical one, something she was able to bypass with two picks and a practiced jiggle of the wrist. Ān-tíng turned the knob slowly and entered the kitchen with one soft step, heel to toe, and then another. She turned the knob before pushing the door closed, then slowly allowed the latch to slide home.

"Hello."

Ān-tíng whirled with her weapon in hand, a stunner she had constructed herself after picking apart an inlari weapon. As her eyes adjusted to the darker interior of the house, she saw her target, Shirrah Opkith, sitting at the kitchen table, his hands empty and held close to his head. The horn structure over his scalp was iridescent in the moonlight, the lattice structure looking familiar and yet foreign.

"No...harm," he said in slow, accented English. "No...hurt."

She kept the stunner trained on him, her heart hammering in her chest. This was supposed to be a cakewalk, one of those missions that wouldn't have threatened her at all. And yet here she was, holding a stunner on an inlari citizen, something that could easily land her in detainment for the rest of her life, if it didn't result in her execution first.

Ān-tíng felt for the doorknob near the base of her spine. It was time to abort the mission and run back to the underground bunker. The prototype could wait for another day.

"Please," he said suddenly in Anshahar, "don't leave."

She froze.

"I see you understand me," he continued. "I mean you no harm, and the comm plate is all the way across the room. You could easily stun me—is that what it is? Clever...You could easily stun me before I took three steps toward the comm to call the *Parhata*."

It was true, and Ān-tíng relaxed a fraction. Perhaps she could escape without being captured. But the *Parhata* would still know a renegade human had pulled a stunner on a citizen. The inlari military police would punish every slave they saw walking alone. Every single Ànchù mission from here on out would get progressively more difficult.

"I just want to talk," Opkith continued. "That's why I waited up for you."

"You knew I was coming," she accused, her lips unused to speaking Anshahar instead of Anshaglish. Her mouth felt as if it were filled with marbles as she spoke.

"I knew the temptation of my research would be enough for them to send someone for it, but my people seem to have forgotten about the human colonies—so much so that they allowed an old man to bring his research home."

"And so you set a trap."

"And so I seeded a rumor, in the hopes that someone would come." His lip pursed in an inlari expression of amusement. "I didn't think I'd have to wait two days."

"Why did you want to talk to me?"

"Not you specifically, but to a human."

"There are humans everywhere in Wellington."

"Not free ones."

That gave Ān-tíng pause. He wanted to talk to a free human? "You could talk to a free human in Australia."

"But not one that's fighting for the freedom of her people."

She didn't have anything to say to him, but swapped the stunner to the other hand.

"Aren't you even curious why I wanted to talk to you?"

"Maybe."

Opkith tilted his head slightly toward the door. "The panel on your left turns on the overhead light. Don't worry. It's not visible from the front of the house, if you want to keep your presence a secret."

She slid the dimmer down and turned on the light. Opkith wore a blue tunic and a dark green robe, his thin legs sticking out from them like two chopsticks, ending in an oddly matched pair of bright socks. He was frail but alert, his light purple eyes looking over her with satisfaction.

"You're here for the research, aren't you?"

Ān-tíng saw no reason to lie. "Yes."

They lapsed into an uneasy silence, and Opkith pointed toward the range. "The water's still hot, if you'd like to make some human-style tea for both of us."

Ān-tíng understood the underlying message: he didn't want tea, but he wanted to offer her tea. And so he offered to drink some of it, to prove it wasn't poisonous. It was a particularly inlari way of handling the offer of a beverage. Ān-tíng considered it. What was his intent in trying to get her to drink the tea?

Her mind whirled, but she finally settled on one thing: he was doing his best to put her at ease. Which, of course, made her even more unsettled. What was he planning to do with her? *To* her? Was she in more danger than Nate?

"Have you seen *Jahama Goes to Australia*?" Opkith asked suddenly, as she walked over with an empty mug in one hand and the stunner in the other.

The play had been written a decade before, and Ān-tíng had seen it four times while perched in the rafters of a theatre catering to the inlaris and their oral storytelling tradition. "Yes," she finally said, returning for the second empty cup. "You're referring to the scene with the two humans in the diner." She had to give it to him—Opkith had a sense of humor. That particular scene featured two humans pointing weapons at each other while trying to eat. It was slapstick comedy on the surface, but was infused with inlari references to the subtle subtext that humans were nothing more than beasts, which imbued a pathos extending far deeper than one would initially expect.

"Yes." He nodded.

She moved the teapot to the table, then brought over the kettle, one hand still holding the stunner trained on him as she did so. She filled the teapot from the kettle, then set the latter back on the stove.

"Thank you."

"The two humans end up dying, you know," she replied.

"It's implied, yes. But it was of their own doing. Still, they had found their *inyata*. It made them more than cattle."

"Love?" Ān-tíng spat out the word in English, sitting down across from him at the table.

"Such a mistranslation," Opkith sighed, shaking his head. "Your human word of love has many facets. *Inyata* is what separates a person from an animal. Some of your philosophers have said that what defines a human from an animal is a belief in God. Others have said that it is intelligence and the ability to rationalize. Yet others have said it's the ability to lie. And still more have claimed that it's the ability to love."

"And *inyata*?"

"One's soul purpose." Opkith smiled, his thin lips spreading into a gentle twist. "*Inyata* can be for child or spouse or sibling or student, or even for a cause, and it changes over time. But the capacity to hold *inyata* marks someone capable of greatness. You, the freed humans...I had to see if you have the capability for *inyata*. Because if you do, then you are not meant to be slaves, and my compatriots on these islands are terribly wrong."

"We were not meant to be slaves," she replied hotly.

"What is your name, child?"

"I'm not giving you my name."

"Are you going to pour the tea?"

She replied by reaching over with one hand and pouring the fragrant tea, so reminiscent of her own childhood in the Ànchù crèche, into each mug. She took the one closest to him.

"So suspicious for one so young."

"I'm not that young."

"So suspicious for one so old, then." His eyes crinkled at the edges as he held the teacup in both hands and took a sip. "What will it take for me to prove to you that I mean no harm?"

Ān-tíng thought. *What would prove that he was willing to be vulnerable?* "Tell me about your *inyata*."

His soft intake of breath was enough to tell her she had hit the mark. He nodded with his horned head at the wall behind her. "The image there. Can you retrieve it?"

She stood, hand still steady on the stunner, and retrieved the flat image in a picture frame. The image surprised her; she had expected all inlaris to have the tiny projectors that displayed 3D memories in brilliant colors, including those that humans couldn't see. "Your family?" she asked, gazing at three inlari children and their mother on a foreign world, their skins flashing iridescent under an alien sky.

"My mother. My siblings." His reedy voice wobbled. "I was

born here, on Earth, but they made the trip here in suspension. They passed through the Deep during the Great War." Ān-tíng guessed from his quiet grief that they had been victims of atrocity. He continued, "They were the reason I had entered the sciences in the first place, to try to find solutions to the problems our people experienced as wanderers. And now that the inlaris are here, I try to solve the problems that would give all of us on Earth a better life—or give us an opportunity to return to the stars."

Ān-tíng hesitated. Was he genuine? Looking into his light, alien eyes, she saw in them a surprising humility, something she hadn't even seen in any of the inlari newscasts so far. She holstered the stunner.

"My *inyata* is our freedom," she declared, setting the frame face-up next to her.

"That's your mission," he replied, "but I don't see more than passion there for you." He smiled suddenly, revealing teeth that were graying with age. "But perhaps I am wrong. Let's talk." Opkith changed the subject in a typically inlari way, with the common Anshahar phrase and a tilt of the head. "What questions do you have about us?"

She took a breath. It was, potentially, the only way she would get any context into the newscasts she had been seeing and the plays she had read. While humans could and did teach inlari culture, a lot had changed in the half-century since humans and inlari had lived in relative peace, and even more had been lost in the years of conflict. Resistance scholars had educated guesses as to the meaning of newly coined phrases, but Ān-tíng constantly felt she was missing some subtext, some secondary meaning in phrases that were ludicrous when translated literally.

"In *Lamasha Cries*, the main character loses a child. What

does she mean when she says: 'The waters run wide, but space always touches the ground'?"

They continued talking well into the night, until yawn after yawn split her part of the conversation.

"I'm not sure you have found your *inyata* yet," he finally said, "but I think you have the capacity. You are still young, child, and one does not find *inyata* easily. Sometimes, it only comes through suffering and loss." When she offered a sleepy protest, he raised a hand. "Come," he offered. "I have a spare room upstairs, and you may use it to rest before you take your leave."

"Thank you," Ān-tíng said honestly, covering her mouth as she yawned violently.

He led her up the stairs to the second floor. "My own sleeping chamber is downstairs, so I don't make it up here very often." The small bedroom at the end of the hall was clean but had the stale air of disuse.

She looked at him intently as he turned to leave.

"My name is Ān-tíng," she said softly. "It means elegant peace. My family wanted peace for our people."

"Ān-tíng," he repeated, pronouncing the Mandarin tones correctly. "What a beautiful name."

She closed the door behind her. She would sleep for half an hour, maybe an hour max, leaving before dawn to return to Ànchù headquarters.

Taking off her boots, she slid underneath the covers and fell into a deep, dreamless sleep.

"Open up, *sabha* Opkith! This is the *Parhata*!" The announcement over the *anlaya* speakers jolted Ān-tíng awake, and she jumped out from under the covers, hurriedly smoothing them down to make the bed look as if no one had disturbed it. She pulled on her boots, zipping them closed, and left the door open as she slid out of the room. She could hear the military police at the door as Opkith spoke to them in a gentle, reasoned tone.

She couldn't hear exactly what he said, but she wiggled into the hall closet next to the heating unit, hoping the heat signature would mask her own in any infrared scan. Despite her uniform, her body would still leave a mild heat trace. All she had to do was keep from sneezing.

As long as Opkith kept her presence a secret.

"We're doing a house by house search, *sabha*, to look for any fugitives. There was an attack on the Central Harbor, and one of the prisoners escaped." The officer's voice was agitated.

Ān-tíng could hear Opkith's voice reply in measured tones.

"I believe there were casualties on both sides, but some of the insurrectionists made it out. We're looking for them now. They couldn't have come far."

Had she hidden her trail well enough? Had she left human hair on the bed? She had forgotten to check. But it sounded like the Holden team had actually broken the General out of his imprisonment. Were they transporting him out of Wellington, out of the North Isle of New Zealand, and across to the the human-dominated Australia?

Her thoughts whirled like the dervishes of old, peppered repeatedly by worries over Nate—Nate, with the front tooth that overlapped the other slightly; Nate, with the goofy grin and the wicked sense of humor; Nate, whose arms had held her against him and kissed her goodbye.

Ān-tíng fought her panic, slowing her breathing and pinching her nose shut, breathing shallowly through her mouth.

"It smells like human," the officer snapped, his voice frightfully near the door.

Opkith's voice was patient, weary. "I rarely come up here anymore. Only the housekeeper comes up here, and she's human. I would expect it to smell like human."

Ān-tíng breathed a silent thanksgiving that Opkith seemed to want to protect her.

The *Parhata* officer didn't respond. Ān-tíng could imagine the officer's silent glare as he contemplated Opkith's response. The sound of boots moved down the hall toward the stairwell, followed by Opkith's quieter tread.

"Thank you for your help, *sabha* Opkith. Stay on alert for the escaped humans; they are considered armed and dangerous." The formal phrasing didn't escape Ān-tíng's notice.

Opkith's voice murmured in response, and Ān-tíng waited until she heard the front door close and lock. She crouched for what seemed like two hours, but was, according to her wrist chrono, no more than twenty minutes.

She sneezed as soon as the knock came, four or five great sneezes that almost caused her to lose her balance. The door flew open, revealing Opkith, a look of consternation on his face.

"It's a good thing you didn't sneeze while the *Parhata* were here," he noted wryly, backing up to allow her out into the hallway. "They went to the neighbor's house, then suddenly ran out and back into their vehicle. I believe it's safe for you to leave now."

Ān-tíng dusted herself off.

He continued, "This is for you, Ān-tíng. I hope it brings you clarity. The encryption key is written on the label."

She accepted the cube and stared at the code in wonder. "Why are you giving this to me?" Ān-tíng demanded.

"I have my reasons," Opkith replied. "Indulge an old man for once. I think it will bring a measure of trust between our two peoples, something that I think we desperately need at this juncture in our shared history." His eyes changed slightly, making him look older, more frail, and, perhaps, a little afraid. "As much as we like to pretend otherwise, there are many things about this universe we inlaris do not understand. Things we may need help with. Things, perhaps, that only humans can help us to grasp."

Ān-tíng nodded, even though she didn't understand.

"Come back in two days if you'd like to talk again. But this time," he chuckled, "come in through the front door. I haven't had a human slave in years, and the *Parhata* may be suspicious if a human doesn't show up every once in a while. The key is under the second flowerpot." He smiled wryly in recognition of the irony of the all-too-human hiding place, his face twisting in an inlari expression so familiar, Ān-tíng almost thought of it as human.

She slid out the back door and through the same hole in the hedge she had entered through the previous day, pausing briefly to clip on the slave collar and pull the white tunic over her head. She took a breath, looked at the street in the early morning light, and quickly scrambled over the berm and onto the shoulder of the road, just another slave on her way to work. As she wound her way along the bay, Ān-tíng could feel the weight of worry beginning to rest on her shoulders, down into the pit of her stomach.

The two questions churned in her gut, roiling as if at full boil. *Was the ansible technology a trap? And was Nate one of the few that had escaped alive?*

Ān-tíng unhurriedly cut through the old reserve that the inlaris had decided to keep in Wellington to remind them of the native flora, just another slave making her way from a common bunk to her place of employment. Had it only been just over a day since she had sat with Nate on their rock in the slave park? The sensations of the new day were almost an assault on her senses, as if her world had been knocked slightly askew by the experiences of the past twenty-four hours, leaving her to consider everything in a fresh light.

After a quick check, she climbed into the storm drain, peeling off her slave tunic and tucking both it and the collar into her rucksack alongside the ansible device. She ran a path through the familiar underground passageways, scurrying to and fro like an animal, pausing every few meters out of habit to listen for other footsteps.

Even here, in the kilometers of passages that were as familiar to her as her own face, her senses felt as if they were on overload. The familiar smell of stale air and the fading scent of washed-away putrefaction almost made her gag at times. The shadows seemed to leer, sending her skittering to the dubious safety of side passages. Time seemed to stand still, and she ran almost aimlessly, her heart pumping hard the entire time.

Finally, she palmed her way into the corridor that led to Ànchù headquarters, stumbling through the convoluted corridor by sheer force of muscle memory before bursting into the large common room. It had been turned into a triage center, with the wounded strewn across the room haphazardly.

Nái saw her before anyone else, rising from where she had been comforting a teenager who was obviously in shock. A medic quickly took over as Nái, her dark, wavy hair pulled back into a rough twist, stepped toward Ān-tíng and pulled her into an uncharacteristic hug.

"Thank God you made it," she said.

"I wasn't on the Holden squad," was all Ān-tíng could say.

"It doesn't matter. The *Parhata* picked up anyone that looked suspicious, and some of those on other missions were stopped and questioned. We're still not sure who was compromised."

"It was a close call." Ān-tíng looked around, scanning through the familiar faces. Some were ashen in pain, others were hidden under compresses and field dressings. "Has everyone returned?"

Nái glanced down and to the side for a moment. When her gaze returned to Ān-tíng, it was laden with the emotional fatigue of leading a company their size. Nái couldn't have been more than thirty-five, but her unlined face, slashed as it was by a deep, white scar, showed a depth of pain that belied her years.

"No," Nái finally replied. "I don't think we'll know who was lost in the blast for another three days, when the team that got Holden makes it to Australia."

Ān-tíng swallowed. So there had been casualties. "Nate?"

Nái shook her head, then simply said, "We don't know yet. He hasn't made it back." She paused, then replied, "Report to Yéh, and then go to bed. You look like hell warmed over."

"Thank you, ma'am."

The older woman squeezed her shoulder and turned back to her original charge, settling the blanket closer around the teen's shoulders.

Ān-tíng shuffled through the motions of writing a report, dumped the ansible into the *hēi-kè* lab, then ambled off to take a shower and collapse into her bunk. Her room was empty—surprising, due to the fact that she shared it with three other women. But perhaps, she thought morbidly, none of them had returned from their missions.

Her dreams tumbled through her mind vividly, a chaotic combination of images that mixed together in an almost incoherent stream. Nate hung from manacles in a dark chamber, screaming amidst the flash of an inlari whip. Opkith, his voice wise, murmured something about suffering and loss, his eyes hooded in the ambient light. Nái and Yéh struggled up a hill, bearing a heavy grandfather clock between them. And Ān-tíng, in a moment of silence, wiped the blood from Nate's chest and cuddled against him as he groaned in pain, his arms wrapping around her in a gesture so natural it made her sob.

She awoke with a start, half sprawled out of the bunk, her weight shifting dangerously off the mattress. Ān-tíng glanced at her chrono. An hour until sunset; she had slept for four solid hours, but it felt like almost nothing. She hurriedly dressed and ran out to the common area.

"Any news?" she demanded of the first medic she saw.

"They're still trickling in," Carlo admitted, his young face drawn and tight.

"Nate?"

"Not that I know of," he replied, shaking his head.

In the lab, she tried to focus on the ansible prototype. The cube fit in her hand comfortably, almost like a softball, her fingers just able to curve around its edges. But Ān-tíng knew she was distracted, unsettled emotionally. The encryption key had allowed her to download the documentation and code on the cube, but all she had been able to do was stare at the words on the screen.

Finally, she tossed the ansible on her desk, picked up her rucksack, packed herself some food, and walked out into the tunnels. She ignored the warnings of danger, knowing she would be perfectly safe in the slave park at night.

She retraced her steps out to the park, slipped on her slave clothing, and clipped the collar around her neck. Someday, she thought to herself, no one would ever need to wear the collar.

Ān-tíng clambered up the steps of the rock, winding her way around the familiar ledge until she reached their spot. She unpacked an apricot and broke it in two, sticking first one half into her mouth, then the other.

She remembered her last morning here with Nate, leaning against him, hands wrapped around a mug of coffee. He had wondered about peace. Was there something to that? Opkith had seemed to think so. She could almost imagine his voice in the liquid sounds of Anshahar as a whisper in the passing breeze:

As much as we like to pretend otherwise, there are many things about this universe we inlaris do not understand. Things we may need help with. Things, perhaps, that only humans can help us to grasp.

This tiny inkling of an idea quickly spiraled into a stream of memories. The quiet laughter she had shared with Opkith at his dining room table as they talked about a confusing phrase in Anshahar. The amazed look on his face as she talked about the conversations she had with slaves—both people who lived under indulgent masters and those who lived under cruel ones.

And then there was Nate, with his thoughtful responses to her emotional outbursts and the way he volunteered his own ideas and feelings in their early morning sessions. Theirs was a connection unlike any other she had experienced before.

But she had also connected with Opkith, she realized. And that, perhaps, was what the Ànchù could really be. Those, like her, who had been raised with the inlari culture, but as free humans, didn't just have the capacity for being weapons. No, they were also capable of becoming *bridges*, spanning cultures and guiding understanding.

The identity settled onto her comfortably with a profound sense of rightness, as if it had always been a part of her. She stared in wonder at the apricot seed in her hand. The seed, like her, had the capacity to grow into something larger than itself. She was uniquely suited to change the world, one conversation at a time. She had found her *inyata*. Her soul's purpose. Her life.

"Ting? I heard you were asking about me, so when I didn't find you at headquarters, I figured you would come here."

Nate stepped onto the ledge and lowered himself gingerly next to her. Her kiss took him by surprise, but he pulled her closer than she had been before, deepening their connection in a way that was both exhilarating and unnerving.

Breaking the kiss, Ān-tíng smiled at him gently, sliding her hand into his. "You won't believe the day I had," she said.

She could hear the wry humor in Nate's voice, his blue-green eyes lighting up with true pleasure. "I can't wait to hear about it."

Ān-tíng leaned her head against Nate's solid shoulder, staring out with an odd sense of peace at the first stars of the dusk as they twinkled over the water. She would tell Opkith later, and they would share a pot of tea, some conversation, and the sense of wonder that came from discovering something new. With her free hand, she slid the apricot pit into her rucksack as a reminder of the moment she discovered her *inyata*.

TRANSMISSION INTERRUPTED

DANA LEIPOLD

108 YEARS AFC

Q UINETTE STROKED ZET's hand with her long, thin fingers as she gazed out over the barren land, sprawling like an unfurled blanket toward the dusky horizon. His hands, so unlike hers, hard calluses against her smooth palm, clasped her fingers with a sense of urgency. His tanned, olive skin contrasted her pale luminescence. They languished as birds in the distance heralded another warm evening and the first stars made themselves known. These moments were precious and harder to steal away as each day passed.

"I wish we could stay here forever."

"Me too." She leaned against his shoulder, careful not to prod him with the elegant horns extending from the side of her head.

He lifted his hand to her cheek, his fingers touching the protruding bones on her face, then tucking stray strands of white hair behind her ear. Her family crest tattooed on his wrist and the silver collar around his neck were constant reminders that their future could never be more than that of a master and a slave. The fact that he had to wear the discipline ring around his neck made her cringe. If she could, she would remove it, but she didn't want to think of what would happen if her mother found out.

She knew the risks when she pulled Zet with her into the pantry and kissed him deeply a mere two weeks ago. The Great Star Inlar must have been shining on her, even though what she had done, and continued to do, was forbidden. All she wanted was to feel something other than the hollow emptiness that had filled her days since her father disappeared. She never dreamed that kiss would evolve into something more, or that she would be sitting with Zet pondering their future.

"We could run away," Zet said.

She lifted her head. "Zet..."

They'd had this conversation before, a few days earlier. It ended with both of them clinging to one another, hoping their separate worlds would fade away. Could she have found her *inyata*? Was it possible?

"I know." He sulked.

She couldn't stand seeing Zet so despondent, so she grabbed his face and kissed him hard, upsetting his balance and knocking him back. He wrapped his arms around her and rolled on top, not realizing they were at the edge of a ridge. They tumbled over the lip. Quinette closed her eyes but never let him go until they landed, and she felt something hard dig into her lower back.

"Kanmar!" Her face contorted in pain as she reached around to feel for whatever had jabbed her.

He sat up. "Are you all right?"

She noticed a silver object poking out from the dirt and picked it up. Adorned with peculiar markings and glistening like a multi-faceted jewel, it fascinated her as she turned the strange item over in her palm. It looked like a cube-shaped, crystal star that had fallen from the sky, and she stared in awe at the mysterious find.

"What is it?" Zet asked, keeping his distance.

"I don't know, but it's...beautiful."

A raised hexagon engraved with rows of interlocking lines in the center caught her attention.

"Be careful. You don't know what it does," Zet cautioned.

"It looks harmless."

She touched the shape, then pressed on the surface, and an indigo light emanated from the various markings. Quinette gazed up from the small object and took in Zet's face. She smiled as the light danced across his features and his smooth scalp. He was both familiar and different. His intoxicating, musky scent made her head spin, giving her a dangerous escape from the loss of her father and a world filled with rules, responsibilities, and obligations. But did they have a future? She knew it was improbable but indulged in the moment as she traced the outline of his jaw with her stare in the azure glow. Then the light flickered off.

"We should get back. I need to prep the meals for tomorrow," Zet said.

"Yes." She sighed.

"What are you going to do with it?"

"I think I'll keep it. It will remind me of beautiful nights with you."

Zet beamed at her, then stood. She tucked the treasure into her satchel, making sure to hide it from view. He helped her up, and she kissed him one last time as they moved in separate directions. Clinging to each other's fingers until the distance between them was too great, they reluctantly let go.

"Wait," he said. "I'll walk you back to the compound."

"I can take care of myself, Zet." She smiled mischievously.

"Yes, I know you are capable, but there have been rumblings in the *Essor*. I need to make sure you are safe."

To ease his mind, she allowed him to walk behind her until they got to the compound's edge. They had to part once they could be seen, since the risk was too great.

"WHERE HAVE YOU BEEN? I ALMOST SENT OUT A SQUAD TO LOOK for you," *Madeer* Valnia Alteiri's tongue clicked against her palate.

Her mother's hands clasped in front of her svelte body, her horns curled into the air like an extended crown, the tips glimmering beneath the hallway's dim lights. She wore a traditional fitted white cassock-style tunic covered by a robe in safflower gold and tied at the waist by a leather weapon belt. An ornate scabbard, which t held her double-edged sword, adorned her belt, and various medals gleamed on her chest.

"Oh, I was...in the fields."

Quinette noticed a twitch in Mother's face and she hoped her lie wasn't the reason. She couldn't stand the idea of another long lecture about dedication to the inlari way of life, which was all Mother seemed to care about. Quinette usually asked her father for guidance when dealing with Valnia, but he had been gone for nearly three weeks, and Quinette had lost hope that Mother's search squadrons would ever find him.

"Really? What about the *Menktun*? Do you feel prepared enough to be wasting time in the fields? You *do* know that this test will determine your future." Her mother emphasized the last few words. "And what about the courting ceremony? Do you think it's wise for a proper inlari to be gallivanting in the fields?"

She didn't want to think about the *Menktun*, the ceremony, or the future. If the future meant becoming a *Madeer* like her mother, with endless military meetings, Governing Council negotiations, and slave entanglements, she didn't want it. Even though she had grown up with slaves at her beck and call, somehow it felt unnatural. She had seen how intelligent and capable humans were at making the most labor-intensive tasks easier. Then there was Zet, deeply compassionate and loving in ways that contradicted the teachings of the Great Star Inlar. Besides, the way inlaris and free humans fought, she wondered if there would even be a future worth living. She constantly wondered why the two species couldn't figure out a way to end the strife. She decided to change the subject.

"Have they found him?"

Mother's face dropped, her round, lavender eyes brooding. Quinette knew she didn't want to talk about Father.

"No."

Mother turned to leave, then stopped and started to say something, her bare brows scrunched together as if she were in pain. She reached out and touched Quinette's shoulder, bowed her head, and walked away.

Bringing up father had worked, like she knew it would, but she didn't expect such a somber reaction. Her intuition told her that Mother knew something about him that she wasn't sharing.

She hurried after Mother until her satchel vibrated. Reaching in, she felt the markings on the box buzzing in her hand. She had completely forgotten about her peculiar discovery, but she didn't want her mother to know about it, so she turned around and trotted to her chamber, passing the porthole windows dotting the stark corridor.

"Mal? What are you doing in here? Shouldn't you be preparing the bath?"

"Mistress!" The slave girl jumped back from behind Quinette's desk. "I...I'm sorry. Yes, I was just straightening things."

Quinette attempted to hide her vibrating satchel behind her back. Mal stared at her for a moment, her shaved head reflecting the light.

"Well! Get on with it then!"

As the girl trotted out of the room, her billowy white pants made a swooshing sound. Looking over her shoulder, Quinette pulled the box out of her satchel and threw the bag onto her sleek desk. She plopped onto her stomach on the bed and kicked off her boots. Turning the vibrating cube over in her hands, she wondered about its purpose. Dancing cerulean shapes on the ceiling illuminated from the small treasure once again, like when she had pressed on the hexagon earlier; but this time she hadn't done anything.

Mesmerized, she hunched over it until an intense pulse throbbed deep in her head. It grew stronger, and she cupped her hands over her ears. The acute pulsation thudded all the way to the tips of her horns, and she dropped the cube and recoiled with pain. The glowing light pounded in time with the thumping. After a few minutes, she couldn't take it anymore. She flung open the terrace doors, scooped up the object, and threw it, still glowing, into the night.

She couldn't sleep. Tossing and turning, she thought of Father—his gentle laughter riding the breeze on their daily walks, his encouraging words whenever she felt inferior, and his dark, violet eyes that held her in such high regard. Why hadn't Mother's search squadron found him? He might be captured and enduring horrific torture. Would she ever see him again?

She rolled over, pulling the sheets tight as she curled into a ball. Then she imagined Zet's soft face, not hard with edges like her own. Such an exhilarating distraction. His inviting lips, his arms enveloping her like a warm pool of water, filling her with a sense of excitement where there had been dread. But he *was* a human. She couldn't pair with Zet—that was forbidden. Inlar would not approve. Quinette imagined the wrath that would come down on her from the Black Star, Rordorah, the bringer of death. Perhaps this was why Father hadn't been found? Was he sacrificed for her misdeeds?

Quinette whipped back the sheets and walked to the terrace. The gloomy sky hung heavy over the compound that was now flecked with large torch-like candles along the pathways. Lakarta had been saving energy resources in response to a command by her mother. Most of the energy cubes were now being used to develop weapons and more sophisticated communications aimed at thwarting potential attacks by human armies. Mother had been tied up in strategic meetings with the Governing Council about some underground resistance threat. Quinette found it hard to keep up, so she tuned out instead. She could never imagine herself as *Madeer*.

Glancing across the horizon, she saw a faint blue glow in the distance: the strange, silver object. It called to her the same way Zet's eyes had the day she kissed him. Would the *Parhata* find it? If so, they would likely hand it over to Mother. Quinette's chest tightened: *She* found it, and *she* would be the one to unlock its mysteries, *not* Mother. She ran to grab her communicator and satchel, then slipped her feet into sandals. Creeping out of her chamber and onto the terrace, she climbed down the twisting vines.

She stayed on the perimeter of Lakarta, using the thick weeds and shrubs as cover. A warm wind blew through her sleeveless nightgown, making the silk billow like a cloud. The *Parhata* strictly enforced curfew at 2100 due to unrest in the *Essor*, so she had to be careful.

The light from her communicator illuminated her steps in the dark. She froze when a shadow wobbled off to her right in the dense red shrub. An animal wandered across her path, stopped and stared at Quinette, then trotted off in the opposite direction. Catching her breath, she glimpsed the fuzzy blue light like a beacon up ahead. Jogging over, she crouched down and reached in, relieved that the pulsing had stopped. She held the silver cube in her palm. Somehow she would figure out what it was and where it came from. Then she would tell Mother, but not before.

In the distance, a thunderous crunching approached. The *Parhata*. Stuffing the container into her satchel, she climbed into the shrub. Branches scratched her bare arms and shoulders, but she curled her body around the bag to hide the blue light.

The massive all-terrain vehicle came to a stop beside the foliage where Quinette hid. The heat emanating from the vehicle almost made her pass out. A few moments later, a squadron of berserkers followed. The gargantuan beasts stood a full two meters, with tusks protruding from their lower lips, making them appear brutish and menacing. They snorted as they each clutched a snapper gun and stood at attention, ready for orders. Seeing them, Quinette shivered. They did the dirty work the soldiers felt too superior to do, which usually meant ripping enemies' limbs off. She held her breath when a berserker sniffed around the shrub. A thin bead of sweat inched from her forehead to her nose, and she willed herself not to move a muscle.

"All clear on the perimeter," a guttural voice shouted above the engine's idle.

"Affirmative. Move on to the west gate," another voice responded.

The berserker huffed, then turned its hulking head toward the ATV. Soon after, the vehicle's tires dug into the dusty earth and sped away as the berserkers shuffled after. Once the squadron was a good distance away, Quinette clawed her way through the prickly branches. She couldn't head west—back to the main compound— and risk getting caught, so she went east toward the *Essor*. Father had insisted on setting aside land for slaves who didn't live with the inlari. Mother had been against it, arguing that it would give humans the opportunity to congregate, but Father's plan for the *Essor* had been approved by the Governing Council. Quinette had been there only once, when she accompanied her father on a good-will visit to bring fruits and linens to the slaves.

Small shacks stood in rows, well past the perimeter of the inlari compound. Thousands of them, each no bigger than Quinette's chamber, had been built out of broken-down buildings and whatever the humans could scavenge off the land. Some shacks looked like piles of garbage so fragile, Quinette wondered how they weathered the storms each year.

Tiptoeing through the slums in the darkness, she stopped to check her satchel. The cube lay dormant, making her wonder what had caused the pulsing and why it had stopped illuminating. After a moment, she continued on and hid behind a large boulder outside the shack she hoped was Zet's. He had told her where it was, but now, in the middle of the night, she wasn't sure. Taking a deep breath, she grabbed a handful of pebbles and flung them at the door. She waited. No response, so she picked up a rock a little smaller than her palm and threw it at the door. Lights flickered on inside, outlining two silhouettes against the plastic windows.

"I'll check on it," Zet said from inside the shack.

He opened the door, and the glow from inside outlined his form. As he stepped into the night, a slight breeze pressed his smock against his lean, muscular frame and Quinette's insides fluttered at the sight of him.

Quinette whistled, a code melody they worked out. He turned his head toward her, then went back inside and shut the door. A few moments later, the inside of the shack went black. Maybe he hadn't heard her? She whistled again. Then the door opened and closed. Footsteps approached, and she peeked around the boulder. Before he could speak, she embraced him and smothered him with kisses. He returned her kisses, then pulled away, holding her at arm's length.

"What are you doing here?"

"Oh Zet, I don't know..."

She reached for him, and he took her in his arms. No matter what inlari law stated, there was something more to humans. Zet was proof. He listened to her laments, he offered hope, and he calmed the angry sea of her mind. A mere *bellogan* could never do that. For a brief moment, she felt at peace, as if all the strife filling her world simply floated away.

Her satchel vibrated once again, but a high-pitched screeching made her fling it to the ground. Zet grabbed his ears and hunched over, protecting himself from the sound. The pounding in her head had also returned. Fearing that they would soon be discovered, Quinette reached inside the satchel and pulled out the cube, which illuminated with blue light, brightening the world around them like the midday sun. She frantically pushed on the box in an attempt to stop it.

"What's going on out here?"

"My father!" Zet gasped.

Uri appeared from around the boulder, his white eyebrows raised. Then a deafening silence fell like an ominous veil over the group. Uri opened his palms, as though pleading for a reasonable explanation.

"I can explain..." Quinette started, but her mind was a blur, so she held out the cube for him to see, "It's this."

He stared for a moment.

"Forgive me, mistress, but I fear for your safety." He bowed, then he turned to his son. "Zet, what are you thinking?"

"Don't punish him. I commanded him to help me," Quinette said.

An ear-splitting shrill came from the cube in her hand, making both Quinette and Zet flinch. Uri fell back and held his hands in the air.

"We must make this stop!" he yelled.

As the screeching continued, lights popped on inside the

surrounding shacks, and alarmed faces peeked through windows. The pain in Quinette's head intensified.

"I don't know how to stop it!" she responded.

"Destroy it." Zet reached for the cube.

"Zet, leave it be." Uri rushed over and seized his son's arm, tugging him away from Quinette. "Get inside."

Quinette grabbed Zet's arm and was about to tell Uri that she would handle this, when the rumbling of massive tires announced the *Parhata* rounding the bend. Blazing headlights cut through the night, and the group was temporarily blinded. She heard the metallic bursts of a snapper gun, and, a second later, Uri lurched. Convulsing, his face contorted as he released his hold on Zet. Time seemed to move like a frozen river as blood splattered Quinette's cheek; Uri slumped to the ground, and Zet's face twisted as he cried out. The mysterious cube, now silent, fell from her trembling hand.

"If you do not want to end up with the same fate, *bellogan*, step away from our sister," a voice boomed.

Four berserkers stomped in front of the headlights, clutching snapper guns, their brawny masses casting intimidating silhouettes. The doors on either side of the ATV opened. Two lanky inlari soldiers jumped out, weaving their way around the line of berserkers.

"Mistress, what are you doing in the *Essor*? Were you assaulted?" a soldier asked.

Zet ran to his father's side. The soldier aimed his weapon and was about to fire, when Quinette rushed in front of the gun.

"I was *not* assaulted!" She could hear Zet's sobs behind her.

"Get into the vehicle. We'll take you back to the *Madeer*."

"I'm not going anywhere." She balled her hands into fists.

The soldier stared at Quinette for a moment, then he held up his wrist and flicked on his communicator. How was she going to explain this to Mother?

"WHAT HAPPENED TO YOU?" *MADEER* ALTEIRI SIGHED, CROSSING her arms, then uncrossing them to wipe the blood from Quinette's cheek. "You used to take pride in yourself and your family. You were honorable and devoted—now you're neglecting responsibilities to spend time in the *Essor*, past curfew, with *bellogans. Bellogans!*"

Quinette sat stiffly in the austere briefing room. She couldn't form the words to answer. Not to *Madeer* Valnia Alteiri, who honored her family and the Great Star with her skill and intelligence. She wouldn't understand. Now Quinette had blood on her hands. *She* caused Uri's death, and now Zet was without a father. She leaned forward, catching her head in her hands, trying to hold back the tears.

"It's been difficult," Mother said, putting her hand on Quinette's back. "But we will prove how resilient we are. We have to, Quinette. There is no other way."

She felt her mother remove her hand and heard the heels of her mother's boots clacking against the floor.

"However, I cannot continue to allow you to dishonor the Alteiri legacy."

Quinette lifted her head. "Mother—"

"Stryoth," Mother ignored her and pointed to one of the soldiers.

"*Madeer.*" He stepped up and saluted, crossing his right hand to his left shoulder. He wore the ornate scabbard and sword high-ranking soldiers proudly donned. His horns curled out from his forehead and swirled under his ears, almost like the noble rams that grazed in the fields. His eyes, purple almond shapes, focused on some unknown point in the distance as he stood at attention.

"I should have done this weeks ago," Mother said to Quinette. "Stryoth, my most trusted *Prala*." Stryoth bowed his head. "You are going to serve as Quinette's full-time escort. You will report to me on the hour of her comings and goings."

"Thank you, *Madeer*." Stryoth bowed his head again.

"No!" Quinette bolted up from her chair, "I do not need a babysitter. I am sixteen. Did you know that Uri is dead?! The *Parhata* killed him! He did nothing to provoke it."

"It's unfortunate." Mother held up her hand.

"What will happen to Zet?" Quinette cried.

"The *bellogan* who prepares our meals?" Mother's brow furrowed.

"Yes! He lost his father!"

"You need to remember how many we have lost!" Mother moved toward Quinette, her aquiline nose mere inches from Quinette's face. "Including your grandfather!"

Mother collected herself and stood up straight, taking in a deep breath then exhaling slowly. "Did *you* know that your father left us for a *bellogan*?"

"What? What do you mean?"

"My search squadron found him in Victoria. He didn't want to return, because he's chosen to stay with a female *bellogan*...who is pregnant with his blasphemous offspring."

Mother's last words struck Quinette like a snapper gun to her heart, "No."

"I know you idolized him, but he's committed the ultimate heresy. He's not who I thought he was, even though he came from a respectable family. It's despicable." Mother leaned over and put her arm around Quinette in an awkward embrace. "So you see, my child, we've all lost our fathers."

Quinette stared at the floor, numb.

Mother released her arm and stood again. She paced the room.

"*Bellogans* are here to serve us! Every day we dishonor the Great Star Inlar when we allow these creatures to keep us from our work. We are the generation tasked with making up for our ancestors' transgressions and winning the favor of our life-giver star, so maybe one day we can return to the star of our origin and be accepted back with open arms." Mother continued her tirade, "I will not stand by and watch you flounder because of your father's downfall. He is dead to us. What's important now, more than ever, is to continue creating one, peaceful society on Earth that pleases Inlar. *One culture, one vision for peace.* You see that, don't you?"

Quinette still stared at the floor, but she raised her head in the silence that followed her mother's diatribe. She met her mother's eyes and nodded.

"Stryoth, take my daughter back to her chamber. She must prepare for the courting ceremony tomorrow."

Quinette hung her head as tears freely rolled down her cheeks.

"One day you'll see that everything I do is for your benefit. My actions may not make much sense to you now, but you must trust me."

THE NEXT MORNING, QUINETTE LAY IN BED, HER HEAD FEELING like a massive boulder that she could not lift. Images from the night before plagued her mind. Flashes of snapper guns, berserkers, blood, her mother's scowl, her father's tender face. She wished she were in Zet's arms, but she knew she would likely never see him again.

Then it struck her. She was like her father: a blasphemer.

Her shoulders shook as she wept.

"It's time for you to prepare, mistress."

Mal bowed at the foot of the bed, breaking Quinette's lament. She turned away, moaning.

"Are you feeling ill?" Mal asked.

Quinette didn't answer, hoping Mal would go away. She stared out the large window to the side of her bed, looking into the compound where other inlaris went about their business, humming along as if the Great Star were shining down on them, none of them aware of her many torments: her father gone, Zet grieving because of her actions, her unwanted destiny laid out before her. Perhaps if she stayed in this bed, her troubles would drift by like a fast-moving storm.

"Mistress, you have less than thirty minutes. I suggest you prepare," Stryoth spoke. He must have been standing outside her door.

"I'm not going."

A momentary silence had Quinette thinking her wish would be granted, until she felt the sheets whip off her body. She turned over to see Stryoth standing over the bed.

"My orders are clear. You *will* prepare and you *will* be at the ceremony on time," he glowered.

Quinette rolled off the bed, slumping like a sack of dried vegetables. Stryoth nodded to Mal and returned to his post outside the door. The slave girl gathered the traditional courting ceremony garments: a violet robe and a golden belt adorned with intricate symbols in Anshahar. Jewels, one white and one purple, designed to fit into two holes they would drill into Quinette's horns, lay on the table near the cabinet. Each jewel symbolized one of the two moons of Inlarah. Mal laid the garments on the bed and went back to the cabinet to prepare a tray of scents to rub over Quinette's body: *glurone* for the cheeks to encourage a fresh complexion, *eruperi* for the neck to give off a pungent sense of power, *zumbeiak* for the abdomen to stimulate the sexual senses, and *biloxia* for the ankles to evoke stability.

"Your suitor will be pleased."

"I hope not," Quinette blurted.

Mal drew in her breath, paused for a moment, then continued working with the scent bottles.

"I see you're ready," Stryoth said, surprising Mal. She turned, knocking one of the bottles onto the floor. The glass shattered into tiny pieces, and the contents splashed Stryoth's boots.

"*Kanmar!*" Stryoth hissed.

The discipline ring around Mal's neck buzzed, her body shaking as she fell to her knees. He held a silver remote control up to administer another shock.

"No! It was an accident," Quinette commanded.

Stryoth glared at Quinette, slowly lowering his hand. "It's time for you to meet your suitor, mistress," he said.

Mal picked herself up off the floor as Quinette moved for the door. "Thank you, mistress," she whispered. Quinette nodded and dragged her feet as she followed Stryoth.

As they approached the receiving room, a heated discussion echoed off the marble walls.

Prala Theede Fendo, from Rimeusha on South Island, sat on one of four *kathedras*. The small stools had been arranged in a circle to the left of her mother. As Theede popped grapes into his mouth, his son scratched the back of his neck, looking stiff and uncomfortable in his ceremonial robe. The younger Fendo's horns were more twisted than hers, the contours of his face more severe. She couldn't name the color of his eyes—they were much lighter than the dark violet of her own. He wasn't as hideous looking as she'd imagined. Several slaves hustled about, delivering traditional fruits on the small silver tables next to each *kathedra*.

"Peace is not possible with creatures who can't even achieve it with their own species." Mother waved her slender hand in the air at Theede. Quinette and Stryoth stood outside the door, waiting for a pause in the conversation.

"We must find a way to work with them. Their forces in Naven are strong," he said.

"We do not negotiate with *bellogans*." Mother shot a glare at him.

"Excuse me, *Madeer*," Stryoth spoke. "May I present to you and your distinguished guests Mistress Quinette Alteiri."

Prala Fendo and his son stood, bowing to Quinette. "I'm pleased to introduce my son, Orkhor Fendo, defender of the South Island Barricade." He gestured to Orkhor, who held out his right hand, palm up. Quinette placed her hand on his, palm down. Orkhor and Quinette bowed to *Madeer* Alteiri and *Prala* Fendo then walked down the corridor to the ceremony room. Stryoth followed and stood outside the doorway. The small room, furnished with only two plush cushions and a table, felt claustrophobic to Quinette. A young slave boy entered the room with a tray. Orkhor, as tradition required, helped Quinette to a seated position on one of the cushions.

"Are you comfortable?"

"Yes." She felt about as comfortable as a slave being shipped off to the Farm.

The slave boy arranged a vessel—a pitcher filled with bright green liquid—and two cups on the table, then stood at attention in one corner of the room. The pitcher held the traditional *somnifera* juice, known to balance male and female sexual biochemistry, and *avena* essence, which calmed the nervous system. Orkhor poured the liquid into the vessel.

"I understand that you're taking the *Menktun* soon," he said.

"Yes."

Her gaze met his as he stirred the juice. His smile, comforting and tranquil, reminded her of the last morning she had spent with Father, when he had asked her what she wanted to do with her life. She quickly averted her eyes.

"Why is such a lovely inlari melancholy?"

His question made her heart ache. She bit her lip in an attempt to keep the volatility inside her under control. What Father had forgotten was that inlaris were all born into their destiny, and nothing would ever change this fact.

Orkhor poured the juice into Quinette's cup and set it in front of her. "It's okay if you don't want to talk. I know this is uncomfortable...I'm also nervous, if that makes you feel better."

She smiled at him and reached for the cup. He placed his pale hand over hers, and she paused.

"What's that?" She pointed to a tattoo on the back of his hand, which was different from the ones used to mark slaves. This tattoo was intricate, with a hexagon shape containing rows of interlocking lines. Quinette had seen this pattern before.

"This?" He lifted his hand, examining the marking. "Oh, it's the sign of the boleeron."

"Boleeron?"

"Yes, the servants of the Black Star."

"Why would you put that on your body?" She scrunched her nose at him.

"To never forget what we have survived and, if given the chance, to carry out retribution."

While he was attractive and seemed kind, his response made her uncomfortable. She had heard Mother speak of the boleeron before and their appetite for destruction. She took a sip of the juice and endured an awkward silence.

The strange, silver object flashed to mind. It had the same markings as Orkhor's tattoo. She tried to remember when she last had it, but if it belonged to the boleeron, she wondered how it got to Earth.

"Quinette, you seem upset. Are you all right?"

"I'm feeling tired. No more drink, please."

Orkhor's face fell. "Have I said or done something to displease you?"

"No, I have to apologize. My mind is elsewhere."

"Is there anything I can do to help?"

If the boleeron were servants of the Black Star, the Rordorah, the destroyer, bringer of death, what was the odd device she had found? Panic spread like a virus in her mind. Though she had never seen one, she pictured the boleeron as gargantuan, with gnarled limbs, large claws, and gaping mouths filled with hundreds of knife-like teeth. Maybe the device was some kind of reconnaissance technology. Maybe millions of boleeron would soon descend on Earth with one goal in mind: the extinction of all life.

"No, thank you. I'd like to go lie down." Quinette raised her hand to the slave boy who stood in the corner.

"Yes, mistress?"

"Please escort Orkhor back to the receiving room. Tell my mother I'm not feeling well."

Orkhor moped as he followed the slave. Quinette stood from the cushion and walked back to her chamber, flinging off the jewels, belt, and robe, leaving only her tunic in place. She heard someone shuffling behind her and guessed it was Mal.

"Is there anything I can do for you?" Mal asked, putting away the garments.

"No."

Quinette sat on the edge of the bed, staring at the floor, rocking back and forth. Mal scuttled away.

"That was rude of you to shun Orkhor."

Quinette looked up. Mother stood in the doorway.

"Mother, I think we're all in danger..."

"What do you mean?"

"I believe I found some kind of boleeron device."

"What? That's impossible." Mother looked as if she had smelled something foul.

"I don't know what it is exactly, but it makes terrible noises and lights up."

Mother put a hand to her mouth, then lowered it, "Where is it?"

"I...I'm trying to remember, but the last time I had it..."

"Quinette, we need to find it." Mother sat down on the edge of the bed, laying her hands on Quinette's.

Then she realized, by Mother's reaction, it must be a reconnaissance device, and the boleeron were actively looking for the inlari. There was a *real* possibility that everyone on Earth *was* in danger. Without filtering her words she blurted out, "Before I tell you, can you please tell me what happened to Zet?" Her heart felt as if it were going to beat out of her chest, and her palms went clammy.

"Why are you asking about a *bellogan?*" Mother pulled her hands away. After a moment, Mother's eyes went wide, as if she had been facing the Black Star itself. "No. You cannot care for him!"

Quinette burst into tears, unable to contain herself.

Mother grabbed Quinette's arms, "Tell me where the device is now!"

"I...I...think it's in the *Essor.*"

Mother activated the communicator on her wrist, "Prepare a transport to the *Essor* immediately."

"Yes, *Madeer,*" a voice responded.

Quinette caught something out of the corner of her eye. Mal had just scrambled past her door.

She grasped against the smooth surface, her legs numb and heavy. There wasn't anything to grip onto, so she pulled herself along, dragging her lower half. The pitch-blackness engulfed her, and she wondered if she had gone blind, but she had to find him. A small shaft of light in the distance grew larger and larger until it filled the vast space and she saw him. His mouth opened, and a scream pierced the air; her head vibrated like it was being sucked into a cyclone. Her body chilled, stiff and brittle like the Icelands she learned about on Naru. Uri appeared in front of him, his back to her, and shook his son; Zet's head flopped back and forth. His warm, brown eyes rolled back into his head until they were white and vacant. Uri turned, a huge hole in his chest revealing bloody ribs and internal organs hanging from his body. She tried to scream, but there was no sound.

Quinette choked for air, opening her eyes. As her breath slowed, she realized she was still in her chamber. How long had she slept? She jumped up to check her communicator: 2018.

A few minutes later, Mal entered the room.

"I'm here to prepare your bath." She lowered her shaven head.

Quinette paced the room, biting on her right thumbnail.

"Mistress?"

Mal. And the bath. Stryoth wouldn't follow them into the bathing room. There was still time before curfew. If Mother wasn't going to tell her what happened to Zet, she was going to find out on her own.

"Yes, yes, yes. I'll get ready," Quinette responded.

Mal helped Quinette disrobe and don a soft cotton wrap. As the slave girl gathered the bath oils and loofah, Quinette grabbed her black tunic and leggings and stuffed them under her wrap. She scanned the chamber for her boots. Opening the closet, she rifled through sandals and other footwear.

"Can I help you find something?"

"My boots—help me find my boots!"

The girl scurried around the room, searching. She found them under the bed and handed them to Quinette, who stuffed them under her wrap, then led the way to the bathing room. Stryoth followed a distance behind them and positioned himself outside of the door to the bath.

As soon as Quinette was sure the door was closed, she dropped her cotton wrap and dressed in her black tunic and leggings. Mal, unaware, placed the oils around the sunken bath in the floor and turned on the water. Pulling on her boots, Quinette shifted her glance to the window facing West toward the *Essor*. Her plan was to slide through the small opening and hopefully fall into some bushes, since it was about a two-meter drop—otherwise it might be a painful landing.

"Mistress, I'm confused..." Mal wrung her hands.

"I need you to keep the water running, at least until I'm out, okay?" Quinette said, pulling the straps tight on her boots.

"I...I don't understand."

Quinette huffed, "I'm sneaking out, and you are going to cover for me. I won't be long. I need to find someone."

Mal helped Quinette off the floor after she had strapped her second boot tight. "Please forgive me mistress, but are you going to the *Essor*?"

"How do you know that?"

"I overheard you talking with your mother...I'm sorry, please don't punish me!" Mal cowered.

Quinette cringed. She would deal with Mal later. Right now she had to get out.

"Stop, I'm not going to punish you. Get on your hands and knees, I can't reach the window."

Mal got down on the floor like a dog, and Quinette stepped on her back. She was able to reach the latch to open the window. With all her strength, she kicked her legs up. She felt Mal push her dangling leg up to the ledge, then she swung her legs so she was sitting on the windowsill.

"Thank you," she whispered, turning to face inside the room.

"Good luck, mistress," she heard Mal say as she launched herself through the window and to the ground.

There were no bushes, and she landed hard on her backside. After catching her breath from having the wind knocked out of her, she dusted herself off and scanned the area. The remaining light of the day was fading fast, so she quickly edged through compound's center and hid behind an ATV parked in front of the Inlarah fountain built to honor her ancestors. Water trickled from the nearly four-meter-high planet at the top, accentuating the falling stars beneath.

Inlari bustled by in groups, followed by their slaves, all hurrying to get inside before curfew. A band of soldiers marched through the square. Quinette tensed as they passed, even though she was well hidden. Once there was a break, she ran toward the fields beneath a forest of kauri trees. She crouched under a massive tree and waited for the sky to turn purple, amber, and then deep blue.

Under darkness, she walked toward the first row of shacks until she saw a silhouetted figure moving toward her. In her haste, she had forgotten to take her communicator or any kind of weapon, so she surveyed the area around her. She spotted a thick branch, picked it up, and held it out, ready to attack. The figure stepped into the faint glow of a half moon.

"Mal? What? How?"

"I went through the window too...I...I thought I might be able to help you."

"You shouldn't be here. Stryoth will find out..."

"Before I climbed out the window, I announced that we were going to do a seaweed treatment on your body to keep your skin supple, and that it would take hours. He won't know we're gone."

Quinette paused and thought this through. She shook her head, about to speak, but Mal spoke first. "Since Uri was killed there have been nightly sweeps every hour by the *Parhata*. We must be escorted to our shacks, even to use the loo. Anything out of the ordinary results in force. I know the *Parhata* follow a specific pattern. I feared for your safety, which is why I came to help you...and, I know where Zet is."

Time was slipping away, and her choices were limited: go back and never see Zet again, or continue on and risk getting caught? If the boleeron were coming, what was the risk anyway? They might all be dead soon. She recalled her father's last question to her:"What do you want from your life?" She wanted to be free, like her father. Free from a destiny that felt unnatural—just as it had felt unnatural to see Zet as a slave. She realized humans were just as capable of *inyata* as the inlari. She wanted to be free to love whomever she chose. And she chose Zet. She didn't know how, but they would get out of Lakarta and live life on their own terms.

Quinette nodded, and they continued. The path became harder to discern, and without her communicator, Quinette could hardly see where they were going. Mal led them to a large building at the eastern edge of the *Essor*. The structure was made of metal instead of salvaged wood, with no windows. Rust covered the dilapidated roof, and the walls had weathered with age and the elements. Quinette wondered if it had been here for centuries. Mal slid the door open, then waved at Quinette to follow. Inside, she smelled musty earth and rotten vegetables, but lack of light offered only shadows and shapes.

"Mal?"

A switch flipped, and bright lights flooded her eyes. Blinking, she could make out a group of humans staring at her. None of them were Zet, only three burly men and one woman.

Mal flashed an unsettling smile at Quinette.

"I don't understand," Quinette said. "What is going on?"

Arms grabbed her from behind. She struggled, but someone pressed a cloth over her nose and mouth—the last thing she remembered.

"What do you think it is? Is it inlari technology?"

"I don't know. I've never seen anything like it before."

The words the men spoke pounded in her temples. When she tried to lift her head, she felt the room spin. She couldn't rub her temples because her arms were tied together behind her back. Her eyes focused on the group of humans across the room. They sat on wooden boxes, huddled around something she couldn't see.

"Someone untie me! I demand to be released!"

Mal rose from the group and sauntered over. She crouched in front of Quinette so they were eye to eye. "I'm sorry mistress, but I can't do that. You are the key to a larger plan."

"What plan?"

"Like I'm going to tell you."

Yelling drew their attention to a commotion outside the building. Mal stood. The screams gave way to an explosion.

"The *Parhata* are here," said the woman across the room.

"Once they discover we have her, they will listen to us," a stout man responded. "Get their attention and let them know!"

The tall man with the beard shoved the door open and stepped into the chaos outside. Mal appeared calm as she turned back to Quinette.

"Where is Zet? He would never take part in something like this. Please tell me where he is."

"Zet is dead."

Quinette's mouth went dry, and the air whooshed from her body in a sharp exhale. "No."

"He and the rest of his family were sent to the Farm. Your mother thought it would send a message to us," Mal said, as if she were trying to inflict the maximum amount of pain with her words. "We received the message. Now your mother is going to have to deal with the Resistance."

"No! You lie!" Quinette struggled to free herself, kicking Mal in the shins.

"Get her under control!" The other woman bounded over to Mal and Quinette. Quinette screamed. She flailed her arms and kicked her feet as the two women grappled with her. Quinette's knee hit the woman in the chest, knocking her down. Attempting to pin her, Mal took hold of Quinette's arms as the other woman recovered and grabbed one of Quinette's feet. A blast shattered the door and part of the wall, leaving a gaping hole. Quinette and the humans halted as a berserker entered.

The two men on the other side of the room threw the boxes they'd been sitting on at the beast. The berserker fired its snapper gun, filling their torsos with metal. Blood splattered across the walls, and the men fell to the ground. Mal screamed, and the berserker shifted its steely gaze to Quinette, who was being held down by the woman. The beast lunged at them then grabbed the woman's right arm, holding the snapper gun to her torso and squeezing the trigger. Mal scrambled to her feet, attempting to flee, but the berserker readied its gun.

"Mistress, please do something!" Mal inched backward.

The berserker paused for a moment, glancing from Quinette and back to Mal. Then he fired. Blood erupted from her gaping wounds, and she fell forward, landing at Quinette's feet with a thud.

An inlari soldier wearing armor peeked into the hole in the wall and scanned the room. "Mistress Alteiri!" He stomped past the bodies and the berserker.

Quinette stared at Mal's body, too stunned to acknowledge the soldier. Her eyes fixed on the blood pooling around Mal. The soldier motioned to the berserker, who sliced the ropes off of Quinette's wrists with its claws like they were thread.

"*Madeer*, Mistress Alteiri is here!" the soldier said into his communicator.

"What?" the *Madeer* shrieked.

"They had her tied up, like a captive."

"I'm on my way!"

Quinette snapped back from her daze and grabbed the soldier's communicator off his wrist. "Mother, did you send Zet to the Farm? Is he still alive?"

"Quinette? Are you all right?"

"Answer me!"

"Hold on. I'm almost there."

Quinette heard the communicator click. The soldier held out his hand, and she gave it back to him. A few moments later, Mother entered the blown out building with two soldiers. She surveyed the room and nodded to the soldiers, who started picking through the rubble.

"I cannot believe they had you tied up! The *bellogans* are going to pay a large price for this act of malice." Mother grimaced when she saw Mal sprawled out in her own blood. "I am thankful to the Great Star that we were close by. We're still looking for the boleeron device. I will have Stryoth executed. He obviously isn't as skilled as I once thought."

"Mother! It wasn't his fault. I left to find..."

"The *bellogan.*"

"You never answered my question."

"Your insect of a father I can accept, but my own flesh and blood? You are betraying everything we believe, everything we've worked so hard to build and maintain...betraying your legacy, your birthright...and me." She paused. "Quinette, how could you? They are savages! You see what they are capable of! They kill their own kind with no remorse. They destroy their own planet without any regard for future generations. If it weren't for us, they wouldn't be here. They would be extinct! And what do we get in return for helping this ignorant species? War. Because that's all they know—how to fight and die."

"I don't believe all humans are like that."

"We are a great race, Quinette, created by the power of the Great Star. Your destiny is larger than the *bellogans* and your infatuation with them. Someday you will see the truth and embrace it, as we all have."

"Excuse me, *Madeer,* I think we found something." A soldier stepped out of the rubble, holding out the silver boleeron device in his hand. He stood at attention next to Quinette.

Mother took the box, picking it up carefully. "We have more important things to worry about now."

"Is he still alive, Mother? Please..."

"Quinette...he's gone. I couldn't lose you too. You left me no choice."

The future she had imagined dissipated from her body like steam from a boiling pot. Her heart broke open, spilling out hopes and dreams and her soul's purpose. Gone. Falling to her knees, she cried out. Gone.

What was left for her? Pairing with Orkhor, bearing his offspring, raising them to please the Great Inlar, and eventually taking her place as *Madeer*? A destined life filled with the responsibility to lead her species back to the ways of her ancestors—a way of life she didn't believe in anymore. And what about the boleeron? Would she have to fight them? More likely, she would live to see her species, and all life on Earth, die in agony.

She felt mother's hand on her shoulder, a dead weight she refused to accept. She got to her feet and pushed her mother away.

"There is always a choice, Mother."

Quinette turned to the soldier and, before he could stop her, she pulled the sword from his scabbard and plunged it deep into her own heart.

Madeer Valnia Alteiri's mouth opened wide, but there was no sound.

BABYLON'S SONG

WOELF DIETRICH

96 YEARS AFC

THEY CAME OUT of the mist. An inlari raid party—usually five berserkers led by an inlari officer. This morning was no different. Armed with cleavers and snapper guns, the berserkers appeared more like the trolls from old fairy tales, with their hulking bodies and yellowed tusks jutting from oversized jaws, and their small, almost dainty, noses. The much smaller inlari officer, covered from head-to-toe in an iridescent armored suit, offered a bold contrast to the massive contingent following him.

They came to kill and plunder and kidnap.

Dawn was a milky orange smear in the distance, and nine-year-old Samantha Babylon ambled along the steep path leading to a small forest behind her family's homestead. Their farmhouse had been built against the southern foothills of the Barren Mountain in New South Wales. Two other families called the valley home, but they were lower and closer to the Bellinger River, about half a day's hike away. The nearest settlement, Dorrigo, home to a couple of hundred people, lay twenty-two kilometers to the east.

Samantha's dad had been a soldier once, in a special unit called the Queensland Devils, until an ionized metal ball from a berserker's snapper gun tore his leg off. Fitted with a cybernetic limb, he retired, and with his pension, he bought their small farm here on the outskirts of the Dorrigo settlement, far away from Queensland politics, and far away from the alien invaders. After the war, people began to move away from cities, preferring to settle in the Outback and less populated areas of Australia, away from the danger another looming war would pose. Although Australia escaped the utter destruction of the Northern Hemisphere, it still paid a heavy price. Cities were decimated. Many millions of lives were lost. Whole families wiped out. The memory of this devastating chapter was still raw and inflamed in the collective minds of its survivors.

A mantle of fog drifted down the slopes, casting gray swaths across the small farm and neighboring valleys. Samantha loved the quiet calm of early morning. Once the sun's might grew and the cicadas woke, their incessant natter would shatter the stillness. Her dad once told her these tree crickets sing because they were lonely, that their peculiar sound was a way of drawing prospective mates, but to Samantha they sounded more like thousands of tiny metal drums, vibrating endlessly, and were just that—noise.

Samantha's jet-black hair, hastily braided, bounced between her shoulders as her booted feet found purchase on the winding trail that disappeared into a clump of trees.

Today she would show her father how good a hunter she'd become, that she could do more than feed chickens and milk goats. Her chores around their homestead felt mundane. She'd rather go hunting with her father than bake bread with her mom. Besides, her younger sister, Kimberley, could help their mother while Samantha explored the forests and creeks surrounding their little farm, maybe even venturing as far as the Dark Forest to the west. There, giant ferns grew taller than a man, and a carpet of moss and lichen made every footfall soft and silent, and the Styx River's icy water disappeared deep into a rocky abyss as if to feed the Earth and mend its sickness. But she knew her dad would have none of that if he caught wind of her plans. The Dark Forest grew too far from their home and posed an unnecessary risk, given that it was not unheard of for an inlari raid party to attack inland. But here, in the shadow of the Barren Mountain, they were still safe and insulated, too deep inland for those aliens to cause any trouble.

Dressed in a loose, taupe-colored fleece jacket and faded jeans and carrying a bow made of ironbark, which she'd been practicing with dutifully for the last two years, Samantha disappeared into the thicket. She carried a small knife on her hip that her dad had forged from an old leaf spring for her birthday a couple of days before. She wore the knife proudly.

She planned to surprise her family with fresh rabbit meat for breakfast. Of course, her mom would make a fuss and chastise her for venturing out alone, as had happened many times before, for if her mom had her way she'd want the girls with her at the house, nice and safe and supervised.

But this new world demanded survival, which meant learning how to survive, and that was precisely what Samantha was doing. Samantha knew her mom's overprotectiveness came as a direct result of her losing her own parents and brother to the aliens. Grandparents and an uncle Samantha and her little sister would never meet because of the murderous inlari. Losing them had had a profound impact on her mother. Samantha did not really understand the depth of her mom's fear, and it felt like a drag when she chided Samantha for slipping out into the surrounding woods, which happened pretty regularly. To Samantha, it felt like her mom wanted to pretend their house was the whole world, a bubble of safety that reality could not penetrate. But then, play-acting was one way of surviving, her dad would say. It created hope, which provided sustenance. Samantha wasn't sure she understood what he meant by that, but if it made her mom smile, then it wasn't a bad thing.

She arrived at a knoll beyond their little forest, a small clearing, which offered an expansive view of the densely treed hills above their property as they melted into the slopes of the Barren Mountain. Copses of red gum and crow ash populated the area, along with pine and red cedar, creating a landscape rich and vibrant with aroma and color and life.

Across the clearing, near a belt of cedars, rabbits skittered into the underbrush, and Samantha traced their frightened hops to the warrens she'd discovered months ago. All she had to do was select a position downwind as close to the burrows as was practical, and then wait. Her patience would pay off if she'd chosen well and remained still and silent. She found a good spot next to a red cedar, near the edge of the forest's boundary. She notched an arrow, squatted on her heels, and waited.

The sky remained hazy and dark, but the mist had broken in patches. Soon the sun would bear down mercilessly and turn the shaded refuge into a sweltering oven.

She waited, listening. Her ears pricked as the rooster announced the day. She'd left a note on the kitchen table so her absence wouldn't worry her folks, not that that would deter her mom's annoyance. But Samantha knew that the payoff would far outweigh her anger. Excitement thrummed deep in Samantha's chest as she imagined their reaction when she brought home fresh meat for stew.

Her father had been teaching them how to survive in the Dividing Range's wild, hostile environment. To Samantha, the huge mountain looming over them and the Nymboida River rising in the northern foothills made this the best place in the world to live. Not that much competition existed out there, now that more than half the world was a wasteland.

She felt alive here. It was a beautiful and dangerous paradise, where the soft wheet-wheet call of the pardalote still echoed in the valleys, and the magpie warbled and caroled with melodious song in the treetops, and the chuckling of the laughing kookaburra sounded more like an agitated monkey than birdsong. And yet, it was the same place where dingoes hunted at night, and the fat-bodied death adder lay waiting under rotten leaves, and the dagger-clawed cassowary battered through the underbrush with its casqued head as it foraged in leaf litter.

Ahead, she heard a soft scratch. A moment later, a rabbit's head peered through the opening of the burrow, ears cocked and snout flaring.

Samantha raised her bow and pulled the string taut slowly, sighting the arrow with its bullet-shaped point on the rabbit, waiting for the gray head to emerge just a little more. She felt the wood fibers quiver in her hand as the small bow strained.

She was about to release the arrow when her mother's distant scream pierced the morning quiet, followed by an explosion that echoed up the mountain slopes and chased birds in a flurry of feathered panic from the treetops.

For a splinter of a second, Samantha did nothing, her weapon still aimed at the space where the rabbit had been. The clashing sounds were surreal and out of place. Another explosion erupted. This time, Samantha turned and ran. Her heart thrashed in her chest as she darted through the trees and underbrush. Branches grabbed at her arms and legs, tearing skin as she rushed down the precarious track, jumping over jutting roots and ducking under low-hanging limbs. Rotten leaves and pine needles muted her footfalls, but her breath wheezed in her chest. Her mind buzzing with panic, she tried to make sense of the screams and cracks below. An icy hand tightened within her abdomen, urging her forward as she sprinted towards home.

The aromatic smell of burning cedar, mixed with the repugnant odor of rotten eggs, filled Samantha's nostrils before the cabin came into view. As she burst through the undergrowth that marked their property, carnage greeted her. Flames and smoke curled up through the cabin's splintered roof and broken windows, spiraling into the sky like some fierce beast consuming their home.

Her mom's limp body lay sprawled across the grassy patch between the burning cabin and the barn. Her four-year-old-sister wailed, frantically tugging at their mother's lifeless body. Her tears streaked the soot coating her cheeks. A huge berserker lay a few feet from them, his face a bloody inverted mushroom, and her dad, using the body as a shield, snapped off shots at four more advancing berserkers. He wielded his old army assault rifle, each shot cracking through the air, as he forced the advancing troll-like creatures to take cover.

Her dad had told her stories about the berserkers, of how the inlari had conquered their planet many eons ago, and how they were enslaved as shock troops and cannon fodder. He also said berserkers knew no fear and acted like utter savages in battle, but nothing prepared her for the reality of their sheer brutality. Almost twice the size of a man, their huge muscles rippled under rough-hewn chest plates and greaves. Each carried a cleaver strapped to his back and a large snapper gun in his hands. The snapper guns reminded her of a blunderbuss, with their flared muzzles and bulky awkwardness.

Samantha froze, her bow tumbling from numbed fingers. Then she screamed.

Her father whirled around, and Samantha witnessed the anguish in his dark eyes. His lips moved, trying to shout something, but a blue light punched through his chest, and he fell forward, his right arm outstretched in front of him as if reaching for her. An inlari officer with shiny armor and a full-face helmet stepped from behind the barn.

"No! Daddy! Dad..." Rooted to the spot, despair and sorrow ripped through her, and she started shivering. Tears streamed down her face, blurring her vision as she tried to make sense of her family home's utter devastation.

The berserkers advanced to where the still sobbing Kimberley crouched next to her mother's body, scanning the yard with their snapper guns and grunting at each other. One of them turned in Samantha's direction, nostrils flaring and beady eyes gleaming with bloodlust, and with a grunt he stomped towards her, kicking her dad's lifeless body out of the way as if it weighed nothing.

Recoiling in horror, Samantha stepped back and tripped over a small knob of earth, landing on her backside. The impact broke her from the shock-induced trance. She jumped up as instinct drove her back towards the forest, her legs pumping like pistons as she ran from the berserker. Her foot caught a protruding root and she skidded on her arms and knees across leaf mold and tree litter. Branches cracked and snapped as the berserker charged after her. Panic crawling up her windpipe, she vaulted onto her feet and continued her mad dash towards the mountain. Despite her knowledge of obscure paths, the berserker gained easily, crashing through obstacles as if they were twigs.

Samantha flew over thick roots and beneath low-hanging branches and shoots, trying to put some distance between herself and the alien. Her heart thundered in her chest. But as the ground rose steadily and her desperate flight to safety took her higher, her legs began to ache from the exertion. The berserker's huge feet sounded like anvils dropping in rapid succession, and Samantha felt the earth shudder beneath her.

Desperation spurred her on, but no matter how much fear boosted her strength, she had no real chance of escaping an adult, never mind a charging berserker.

The beast's ragged breathing huffed behind her, and Samantha glanced back. In that one brief moment of looking back, her foot caught the edge of a dingo hole, throwing her off balance, and she crashed to the ground.

By some miracle, she didn't break her legs, but the fall winded her. Her eyes wet with tears, Samantha couldn't even muster enough breath to cry out. Her diaphragm felt stuck, and a stabbing pain shot through her chest as she gasped for air.

The berserker tore passed her, missing her by a finger's breadth. Tripping over his feet as he wheeled his massive body around, the creature tumbled backwards into a huge cedar trunk, grunted from the impact, and careened into the underbrush, unable to stop his momentum. The alien thrashed as he tried to free himself from the tangle of broken twigs and torn-out stems. Enraged, he barked at Samantha—a muffled, guttural sound that sent a spike of ice down her back.

Panting, Samantha wriggled backwards into the narrow dingo hole, pulling her knife from the sheath. Bushes snapped and crackled as her pursuer struggled towards her. Her heart jumped in her throat, fear rolling over her in waves and twisting her body into spasms of terror. She wanted her dad. She wanted to get back to him. *He's not really dead*, she told herself. *He'll protect me. I just need to get back to him.*

Kimberley!

Kimberley was still at the cabin. Samantha's body shook as grief and fear brought fresh tears.

A heavy boot crunched over strewn twigs, followed by laborious breathing. A shadow fell over the small entrance to the hole.

Dropping to his knees with a harsh laugh, the berserker shoved a muscular arm into the hole, clawing dirt and stone in the process. Long, chipped nails grabbed at her, with fingers almost as thick as her wrists. Samantha slashed at the ugly hand, the honed blade biting into the vulnerable webbing between the fingers. The berserker yelped and jerked back, shaking loose clumps of the interior wall. Dirt rained down on Samantha as the hole caved in; dust stung her eyes and blinded her. A string of unintelligible barking followed, and then the rasp of metal on leather as the alien unsheathed his cleaver.

SAMANTHA SAT ON A NARROW METAL BUNK WITH HER BACK AGAINST

the wall of a small windowless cabin. Her dad used to call these submersible vehicles ASVs when he'd told stories about how the aliens would come ashore to kidnap humans. Afterwards, he'd assured her their cabin was too far inland—that they had nothing to worry about. To Samantha, the ASV resembled more a giant manta ray than the traditional oblong submarine humans used to use.

The only source of light came from an LED strip above the cabin's narrow door. Kimberley lay asleep on her lap, her dark hair tangled and wild across her face. Emotional trauma and hours of wailing had taken their toll. Depleted, she'd dozed off.

The Thompson sisters—three teenage girls from a neighboring farm—huddled on the opposite bunk. Their older brother wasn't with them, which Samantha took as an ominous sign. Haggard and dirty, the girls' clothing hung in bloody strips. In the gloomy light, their eyes shone vacantly, like they'd stopped noticing the outside world. Their parents must have been murdered too, she realized. And they hadn't been the only group. Another inlari raid party had been waiting onboard the ASV when they reached the river. Samantha had heard whimpering emanating from two other cabins just before she and her sister were shoved into theirs.

The inlari officer's timely intervention had saved her life back in the forest. Furious, the berserker had plucked her from the broken hole, his ugly cleaver poised for killing. She shrieked, but then the inlari officer had appeared out of nowhere and ordered the berserker to stand down. Thin and lithe like a panther, the officer barely reached the giant creature's shoulder.

The officer's metal armor and helmet glimmered like the shiny insides of a shell as he reached for her wrist and squeezed. Her fingers popped open and she dropped the knife back into the broken hole. Speaking in a language Samantha didn't understand, the inlari barked at the much larger alien, and he reluctantly sheathed his cleaver and tossed her over his massive shoulder. They returned to the cinders of Samantha's home, leaving behind her dad's last gift to her.

Nothing but smoke and embers remained of the cabin. The barn, too, lay in ruins. Her parents' bodies were unrecognizable, charred and grotesque. Seeing what was left of her parents, Samantha screamed. She screamed until her throat burned and her chest ached, and only silent tears remained.

They were almost at the river when she saw an unconscious Kimberley slung over the shoulder of another berserker. She shouted Kimberley's name, but her voice came out hoarse and grated raw in her throat. She squirmed and pushed against the alien, but a giant hand held her legs tightly. Exhausted, she gave up.

That had been many hours ago. Samantha couldn't tell time anymore. Everything seemed a daze to her, unreal, like a series of horrific images she couldn't escape.

Her eyes wet from fresh tears, the shock of losing her parents had taken something from her. Mentally exhausted, she couldn't muster enough strength for even fear, and numbness set in. She peered down at her baby sister and carefully pushed the hair from her face. Dried mud and soot streaked Kimberley's cheeks, and an ugly bruise darkened the side of her face. Her eyelids twitched with restlessness. Samantha stroked her face and whispered sweet things. Things she knew were not true anymore. Things she did not believe, that no longer existed. After a while Kimberley's breathing fell into a rhythm, and her face softened.

Watching her sister's serene face, the thin shell of numbness cracked, and new tears swelled in Samantha's eyes at the thought that this was a temporary reprieve only. As raw emotion surged through her, Samantha wept with loss and regret and shame. Shame that she had caused her father's death and deserted her sister. A terrible anguish threatened to tear her apart as she strained to keep her sobs from wracking her body.

LEFT ALONE WITHOUT FOOD AND WATER, SAMANTHA'S STOMACH growled in protest. Her tongue felt thick and rough with thirst, but she tried to ignore the discomfort. She didn't deserve water anyway, not after abandoning her sister the way she had and getting her dad killed. Misery was her penance.

But what about Kimberley? She was only four years old.

The cabin door clunked open, and an inlari officer entered, the same one who had murdered her dad. He still wore his armored suit, but no helmet to hide his horns. Ribbed, brown, and swept back from his forehead in a majestic swirl, they resembled a ram's, only smaller. His lean face boasted high, sharp cheekbones, and his eyes narrowed to slits as he glared at them.

"We are almost at our destination, humans. When we disembark, do not attempt escape, because there is no place to escape to. From here on out, you listen to what your masters tell you. Failure to obey will result in punishment. Severe punishment. Is that clear?" He studied the girls, his eyes lingering on each one. "And wake up the little one!"

Samantha cuddled Kimberley to her chest as if the mere act of doing so would protect her little sister from their fate. Startled, Kimberley howled again. The alien ignored her, but before he left, he paused and looked back and gave a half-smile. "Welcome to Lakarta." The door clunked shut behind him.

The Thompson girls sobbed, and Samantha held Kimberley tighter, her baby sister's fear rattling both of them.

THE SUN DIPPED IN THE WEST WHEN THEY REACHED WHAT SHE guessed was the Port of Auckland, only the area had been renamed to something she couldn't pronounce. Two berserkers escorted Samantha and the girls to the deck of the ASV.

Kimberley held on to Samantha, the knuckles of her little fists white as she clenched the fabric of her older sister's tattered fleece jacket. Samantha wrapped her arm around her as they trudged down the gangplank behind the Thompson sisters and onto the pier where another haggard-looking group of girls waited.

The port was a bustling mess of confusion. Inlari and berserkers mingled with other humans as they conducted their business. Traditional forklifts transported huge containers and unknown goods, and a variety of oddly-shaped vehicles painted blue or yellow blustered through the streets and around the wharves. Samantha had seen cars and bikes and other powered vehicles in Dorrigo, but they never looked this new and shiny.

With the aliens calling New Zealand home and being at odds with humans in Australia, Samantha wondered how they even had a busy port. The humans here differed in shape, age, and size, but they all had three things in common: shaven heads, white tunics over white loose-fitting pants, and a thin silver collar around their necks.

They were ushered towards a procession of inlari military vehicles with matte black exteriors and blackened rims when a berserker tore Kimberley from her grasp, grabbing a fistful of the little girl's hair. Samantha reached for her, shouting Kimberley's name as her sister shrieked, but the inlari officer stepped in and swatted her across the mouth.

Falling to her knees, she tasted blood, and tears welled up in her eyes. Kimberley's anguished screams echoed in her ears, and Samantha pushed up again and called after her. She tried to shove past the officer, and he hit her again, sending her sprawling onto the bleached concrete surface of the wharf. Through dizzy eyes, she saw the berserker toss her shrieking sister into the back of a yellow vehicle and shut the latch, muting Kimberley's wails of pain and horror.

"I warned you, human. You are property. Your duty is to obey. Nothing else."

"She is my sister!" Samantha cried. "She is my sister! You can't do this. Please don't do this. Please let me go to her. Please!"

Ignoring her pleas, the officer's face remained impassive as he produced a baton the size of his fist. He twisted the end of the stick and three cords shot out, crackling with pulsing blue light.

Samantha shielded herself the only way she could, by lifting her arm, but the first lash curled around her forearm and tore through fabric and skin. She screamed and turned away reflexively to protect her injured arm, inadvertently exposing her back to the alien. Four more lashes cut into her back, hips, and shoulders before Samantha could roll away. Her body blazed with agony as blood soaked her shredded jacket. She sobbed and whimpered, calling out to her dad to help her. Another lash ripped into her raw back, and Samantha lost consciousness.

HER DAD MADE FACES, MIMICKING THEIR MOTHER'S STERN expression after she'd reprimanded Samantha for skipping her chores earlier that day.

Her mom shook her head in mock disapproval of her dad's escapades, and Samantha and Kimberley laughed. Her mother's freshly baked bread filled the air with a sweet aroma that mixed well with the fragrance from the old wood burner and roasted coffee beans.

Her dad's dark eyebrows twitched and his forehead wrinkled as he laughed. Gray streaks colored his bushy beard and his teeth shone like white marble, but then he glanced at Samantha and turned serious.

"Still, there's a place and time for everything, Sam. Your mom is right about you needing to do your chores. You can't skip them. There's plenty of time for practice with your bow and for exploring afterwards. Remember, it's about keeping balance."

"But Dad, everyone needs to be able to fight and survive. I'm much better at shooting my bow than feeding chickens." Her voice pled in earnest.

Her dad smiled. "Yes, but who will feed the chickens then? Besides, your mom can't do all the work. That wouldn't be fair, eh?"

"No, it wouldn't," Samantha answered slowly, lowering her gaze.

"Don't look so gloomy," her mom interjected. "No one is angry at you."

"Thammy is thad!" Kimberley shouted, her face puckered with concern for her older sister.

"No, she's not." Her dad winked at her. "She just doesn't like being wrong. She's like her dad in that regard."

Samantha's face lit up then, and she broke a piece from the fresh, still-warm bread and took a huge bite.

Kimberley laughed.

A WEEK PASSED AS HER INJURIES HEALED. THE ALIENS ALLOWED her wounds to fester for three days, probably as a reminder of the cost of disobedience. They then injected her with a serum that accelerated skin repair, fought infection, and, mercifully, numbed the pain by cauterizing the nerve endings—or that is how the female inlari who administered the injection had explained it to Samantha. She was kind and her voice soothing as Samantha battled through fever. She also told Samantha that the serum did not prevent scarring, and so Samantha's first introduction to Lakarta left her body with a permanent reminder.

She soon departed the medical wing of Lakarta Detention Centre for the dormitories. Tiered bunks filled a huge room at least six rows deep, but only one row was occupied. As though cast from a mold, the blindingly white walls were smooth and free of any seams or switches or indents. The toilets and basins were situated at the one end of the room; the dulled metal smelled of vile disinfectant, which made Samantha gag. A series of caged fluorescent panels dangled from chains below the rafters and illuminated the dormitory with a harsh light that made her skin appear yellow. Fear clung to the girls and hung like a heavy fog over the room.

Sometimes, in the middle of the night, when the children's whimpering and weeping ceased, when Samantha's own thoughts were at their darkest, she focused on the low buzzing sound of the fluorescent tubes. The noise reminded her of the cicadas back home. And so, at times, when her fear and sorrow felt the heaviest, she would close her eyes and pretend to feel the mountain breeze on her skin as she lay in her bunk. She imagined that the yellow lights glaring behind her eyelids were the sun's warm light beating down on her, and above her, buzzing with abandon, the cicadas called to be rescued from their loneliness. She missed those noisy tree crickets and wished she'd never spoken ill of them. What she would give to hear those insects and their weird songs of longing once more.

Foreign-tasting gruel, which reminded Samantha of mushed cardboard, was served as their meal twice a day and gave Samantha diarrhea the first week, but she got used to it quick enough, and her body adapted.

She heard stories by eavesdropping on conversations from the other girls, but these tales were more like whispers and speculation, made more frightful by stories of cruelty and of sexual abuse by the aliens.

Each morning, the same inlari female would pay the girls a visit. The pale-skinned alien wore a cassock-style blue tunic with yellow and white trim, but instead of a mandarin collar, the tunic had a v-cut with some kind of tight-fitting white undergarment. Her dark horns jutted from her forehead like a billy goat's and were smooth and thin, smaller than the inlari officer's. She kept her shoulder-length white hair tucked behind her ears, and her thin eyes gave her an almost elvish appearance.

"*Bellogans*," she would say in heavily accented English, "your presence here is to serve as property of the great inlari nation. In that alone, there is honor far above your station. Some of you, if the Great Star should bless you with good fortune, will be chosen to serve as concubines for one of the higher houses. This position brings with it some comforts and freedoms you would not ordinarily enjoy otherwise. It would be in your best interest to pay attention when spoken to and show respect to your masters. Always obey instructions. Failure will result in punishment, and punishment will diminish your chances at finding 'good fortune' here in Lakarta." She would say the last line with a smirk on her face as she weaved between the bunks, hands clasped behind her rigid back.

With each day's visit the same message was repeated. Over and over again. None of the girls ever questioned her, and they listened attentively, eyes wide with fear.

"To help you adjust to your new life, you'll be fitted with a discipline ring. If you disobey a command, the ring will punish you. It will hurt. If you try to escape Lakarta, something worse will happen. Do you understand?" Shocked faces would stare at her in horror and nod. Some girls cried.

This speech became a fixture of the mundane routine at the detention center. The only other visitors were human wardens, women dressed in white overalls with red arm bands, who came to select the girls and whisk them away to a predetermined destination. At first, they were relieved to see a human adult, but the female wardens ignored their questions and shouldered them out of the way. They learned to fear the silent wardens, viewing them as harbingers of doom. Each day, two or three girls left. The fear in the dormitory was palpable and toxic and constant.

Samantha met Carik during her second week in captivity. Until then she had kept to herself, occupied with thoughts of her baby sister. Carik was her own age, but where Samantha had raven hair, now shaved to stubble, and dark eyes, Carik's eyes were the color of blue ice and her white-blond hair fell in unruly curls over her shoulders and back. Carik had been earmarked for one of the higher houses on the first day of her arrival. The inlari had already branded her with that house's sigil.

"Do you want to see my tattoo?" Carik asked one night. She slept on the bottom bunk.

Most of the girls were numb from loss and terror by now and availed themselves of light banter, though a giggle or laughter was a rarity.

"Sure." Samantha had answered, not sure what else to say, and Carik rolled from her bunk and pulled up her white tunic sleeve, revealing the small blue tattoo on the inside of her forearm, just below the fold of her elbow. Samantha could make no sense of the sigil or "Coat of Arms" as some of the other girls had come to call it, for it looked more like hieroglyphic patterns that had been squashed together to form a rough square.

"What does it mean, do you know?" Samantha asked, studying the weird shapes and patterns.

"I don't know," Carik answered. "It's really pretty, and it didn't even hurt. Put your finger here. You can feel it. It feels weird." Carik giggled as she offered her arm to Samantha, who touched the welted mark hesitantly. The edges were smooth and slightly warm to the touch.

"They told me I'm going to be a concubine."

"What's a concubine?" Samantha asked. "It sounds like porcupine."

They both laughed.

Neither one was yet sure what being a concubine entailed, but the female alien had told Carik the position included comforts, which, to their minds, was better than being beaten or worked to death.

"Have they chosen you yet?" Carik asked. Her eyes were bright and innocent, her curiosity desperate.

"Not yet. Next week maybe. I don't know." Samantha played with the seam of her tunic, studying the white zigzag stitch. Her mother used to make their clothing, and she had taught Samantha how to sew and stitch. Samantha hated it and always ended up pricking her finger.

"I'm glad they took me, you know." Carik said. "I lived with my uncle, but he was a bad man. He hurt me a lot. Now he's dead."

Samantha looked up and studied Carik's face. Her eyes were so big, but Samantha saw fear there. Carik's bottom lip quivered as she tried to show a brave face.

"I don't think this will be better. You've heard the stories—"

"Do you know where you'll go?" Carik asked quickly, ignoring Samantha's words.

Samantha shook her head. "No, not yet."

"It's a surprise then." Carik smiled.

Samantha didn't smile back and wondered if Carik was right in the head.

They came for Carik the next day. On her way out, she turned to Samantha and smiled, waving to her as if this was an ordinary everyday thing and she was bidding her farewell.

Samantha did not wave back and just stared after the girl, thinking how odd it was for someone to be so lighthearted in the face of such unspeakable horror.

She was too numb to care either way.

BY WEEK THREE SAMANTHA HAD STOPPED CRYING. HER THOUGHTS still dwelled on her sister's lot and the loss of her parents, but she'd developed a detachment from her surroundings. Samantha viewed her new life from behind a mental barrier, where she was just a passenger in someone else's life. She would still wake up at night from time to time, cold sweat pearling on her forehead, but being awake now became a reprieve, where sleep used to be an escape.

During week four they came for her. The two human wardens that had taken Carik, dressed in their white overalls and red armbands, and escorted Samantha from the room. She didn't protest or fight them.

The detention center consisted of a main administrative building and eight dormitories, four on each side of the main building, attached by an external hallway. They led her to the administrative block, where a stern-looking inlari female with long black hair and oddly-shaped horns processed her. The alien had a name tag on her chest, but the letters were written in inlari, and Samantha couldn't read it.

The alien stood up from behind her desk and beckoned Samantha to come closer.

Samantha obeyed, shuffling forward.

The alien fitted a thin silver collar around her neck. Next, she took Samantha's left arm and pushed up the sleeve. With a coil-like machine, she tattoo-stamped Samantha's arm below the curve of her elbow. It was quick, but it hurt. Carik had lied to her about not feeling a thing. The tattoo was slate gray and edged, and, as with Carik's, the image made no sense to Samantha—just a bunch of lines and triangles meshed together in a rough square. Samantha traced her finger over the welts absentmindedly and saw the coloring change to a dark blue, like the color of blueberries.

"Are you listening, *bellogan*? As I explained, *bellogan* is what you are now. That is what we call human slaves."

Samantha looked up and found the alien glaring at her.

"I'm sorry." Samantha gazed down again at the tattoo on her arm, softly stroking and feeling the tiny contusions made by the fresh ink.

"Pay attention! Your new name is Bol. You will respond to no other name. Using your human name is forbidden and subject to severe punishment. Do you understand?"

"Yes." Samantha replied.

"Yes what?" The alien snapped.

"Yes, I understand."

"Now say it. Say your name." Spittle foamed at the corner of the inlari's mouth.

"My name is Bol," Samantha mumbled, irritation flaring in her eyes.

"You'll be working as housekeeper for the Zocht House. Your master is Ledik Zocht. Address him as Master Zocht. Work hard and obey the rules. If you become useless, either through injury or sickness, you'll be sent to the Island. Do you know what that means?"

Samantha shook her head.

"Of course you don't. That is where they terminate unusable slaves before they waste our resources."

"Or you could just not kidnap us and leave us alone," Samantha replied.

The inlari studied Samantha for a moment and then smiled at her, but the smile did not reach her eyes. A surge of electricity shot through Samantha's body, causing her muscles to spasm, and she dropped to the tiled floor. Samantha clawed at the collar, but it burned her hands, and she screamed out in pain. Tears flooded her eyes.

The alien lifted her arm, and in her hand Samantha saw a small silver disk. "Do you have anything else to say?"

Samantha sat up and wiped the tears from her face with shaking hands. Her muscles ached. Prickles still ran down her skin. She shook her head slowly. Moving was excruciating.

So far she had succeeded in surviving by locking her emotions away, but being electroshocked crumbled her resolve. Her guilt and shame burst through like a great avalanche of emotion. She bit back the tears and tasted blood on her lip.

Samantha's shoulders shook with a sorrow that ran so deep, it went beyond the cold comfort of self-pity. It was a sorrow fueled by guilt. She had caused her dad's death and abandoned her sister. She should have done more. Maybe if she hadn't distracted her dad, he would now be alive. He could have saved them from the aliens. .

And yet, a spark of hope lingered—hope that her sister could still be alive—and maybe they could be reunited again, maybe even escape this wretched island. Her dad had told her hope was important and that hope helped you survive. And she would do that. She would hold onto that hope of finding Kimberley.

"Bol, follow me." The inlari female came out from behind her desk and walked through the office door to the foyer, expecting Samantha to follow her.

Samantha struggled to get up and limped after the inlari, her legs rubbery.

The foyer was small and sparsely furnished, with a solitary receptionist counter opposite a set of double doors that served as entrance to the administrative building. Sunlight streamed through the open doors and windows and turned the smooth white-tiled floor into a mirror.

A female inlari stood behind the counter, preoccupied with a digital screen. She too had long dark hair that lay loose about her shoulders, and her horns were similarly short.

The alien who had processed Samantha greeted a male inlari who stood just inside the entrance.

Samantha's hands were clasped in front of her, and she approached them with her head bowed, eyes on the floor, for fear of provoking another admonishment.

They spoke in their inlari language; the sounds were smooth and melodic. Samantha, of course, did not understand a word. She stood quietly while the male appraised her.

He wore a cassock-style tunic the color of sea sand with dark brown trim on the cuffs and lapel, and, like all inlari Samantha had seen thus far, a tight-fitting white bodysuit underneath.

"You are Bol," he said in English. "I am Master Zocht."

Up close, his horns were majestic, the way they curved from his forehead and swept back, ending in another swirl at the nape of his neck. His skin was tanned and his narrow eyes a brilliant blue with creases at the corners. They were kind eyes, something Samantha had not yet encountered. Like most inlaris, he had an angular face, and it was near impossible to determine his age. Instead of the usual thin inlari lips, his were full, almost feminine. Faint lines at the corners gave the impression he laughed often.

"I am." Samantha answered as politely as her fear allowed her. Her body trembled. Unsure what else to say, she remained quiet.

The female alien frowned at her and was about to say something when Master Zocht intervened in English again, "I will take it from here, Matron Salek. May the Great Star embrace you in Her holy light."

"And you, Master Zocht." She nodded respectfully, gave him

a small white satchel containing the remote to Samantha's collar, and retreated back to her office.

Master Zocht turned to Samantha and studied her face wordlessly. It made Samantha uncomfortable and she shifted on her feet.

Seeming satisfied, Master Zocht smiled and said, "Come with me, Bol. Let me take you to your new home."

MASTER ZOCHT'S OBLONG-SHAPED CAR HAD SIX WHEELS AND WAS painted a metallic orange. Like all vehicles on Lakarta, as Samantha would later learn, it was powered by the inlari's infamous power cube technology. The vehicle's interior showed orange and white trim and an array of high-tech panels with no discernible steering wheel. The edges of the dashboard curved downwards smoothly and formed part of the two front seats, creating a cocoon-like cockpit. The dashboard lit up brightly when Master Zocht climbed in, turning the large windshield into HUD. Both armrests had small panels at the ends, and these pulsed with blue and red lights. Master Zocht placed his hands on them with his fingers splayed apart, and the engine whined into a high-pitched hum before settling into a soft purr. Samantha felt a slight vibration under her feet as the vehicle moved forward.

"Unfortunately we are forced to use old technology, resources being limited as they are." Master Zocht snapped a quick smile at Samantha. "We still have hovering transports, but they are not as widely used."

Samantha nodded slowly, but she had no idea what he was talking about. It seemed best to remain quiet.

They drove from the harbor and turned onto a road that

slowly rose higher, giving Samantha an expansive view of the port and surrounding areas. Most homes were still human-designed, like the pictures she once saw in an old yellow-paged magazine. Classic villas to flat-roofed art deco styled houses built from either weatherboard or stucco and concrete blocks lined the streets. Some large, others small. Some must have dated back more than a hundred years. Apart from a few road signs in the alien's language, this part of New Zealand seemed very human-like.

Master Zocht did not speak to her during the remainder of the drive, and a strange calm descended on Samantha, and she relaxed a little. Her ever-present fear seemed to have settled to a manageable level, so she sat back and watched the houses, gardens, busy shops, and aliens walking around in colorful gowns and tunics. Unlike the port, there were no color limitations here.

The drive was not a long one, and they reached their destination barely thirty minutes after leaving the port. Samantha's heart thumped in her chest, and she felt the icy claws of fear prick her skin when they turned into a gated property with a long driveway.

Master Zocht's home was situated in a suburb called Half Moon Bay. The house was on top a hill and overlooked a marina and Auckland's Sky Tower to the east. His home was grand and luxurious and, again, decisively human made.

He parked the vehicle in front of a double garage. "Please follow me, Bol." Master Zocht said as he got out and opened her door.

She was taken aback by how gentle the alien treated her. How kindly he spoke to her. It confused Samantha, whose hatred for the aliens had increased tenfold since her kidnapping. She saw no humanity in them. No love. No decency. Just a rigid class system based on abuse. Master Zocht's kindness contradicted her experience.

She climbed out gingerly and followed Master Zocht as he entered the house. Samantha saw him place the satchel, which held the remote to her collar, on a small table at the entrance hall's far endl, and some of the tension left her. She exhaled audibly.

The residence was a modern structure with six bedrooms and seven bathrooms spread out over three levels. Samantha had never seen such splendor before. Her mind struggled to make sense of the extravagance of it. The living room opened to a roofed deck, a sprawling green lawn, and a tropical garden. The vista offered from the deck was mind-numbingly beautiful, and Samantha struggled to reconcile her treatment and the nightmare of her loss with such beauty. It made no sense to her. How could such opulence also represent such cruelty?

"It is beautiful, is it not?" Master Zocht said behind her.

Samantha whipped around, her meandering thoughts gone, and tension seeped back into her bones as she watched the alien warily.

"Do not be afraid." Master Zocht smiled, and the smile danced in his eyes. "I'll not hurt you. You will never be hurt again for as long as you remain in my service."

His words surprised her. They clashed utterly with her newly created life narrative amongst the inlari. She felt relief pushing against her resolve, threatening the brittle wall she had built around her emotions. She desperately wanted to believe him.

"I don't understand, Master Zocht." Her voice trembled. "I'm to be your slave, am I not?"

The alien gave a short laugh and smiled at Samantha. "Officially, yes, but unofficially you'll be my...student."

"Can't I go home, please?" She blurted out. Her voice was thick with emotion. "Please! I won't tell anyone, I promise. Please let me go home."

Master Zocht's expression softened and he shook his head. "I'm sorry, Bol. That is not possible. This is your new home now. You can never go back."

"What about my sister?" Samantha pleaded, her eyes big and hopeful. "Can you make Kimberley your student, too? Please?"

Master Zocht stepped closer and gently placed his hands on Samantha's shoulders. She was shaking. She did not wince or step back from him. Instead, Samantha stared at him with a mixture of sorrow and hope so intense, it bordered on insanity.

"I cannot, Bol. Someone of my station is only allowed one human slave. I chose you because, unlike the other girls, you did not share your tears with the world. I saw great strength in you. Your species fascinates me, and having you here will be a wondrous opportunity to explore human nature in detail. I will teach you about inlari society, about our culture and our norms, and in return, you will teach me human nature." He gave Samantha another smile and then squeezed her trembling shoulders, as if his words could soften her loss and wipe out the memory of her sister.

"As for your sister, it's best you forget about her. Like your human name, she is now in your past. It is better this way. Trust me."

Samantha stepped back from the alien and fell to her knees, shaking. Tears stained her cheeks in great rivulets. This one moment of hope, of seeing a light at the end of a dark tunnel, had been significant enough to break down the emotional wall Samantha had carefully constructed around the brutality of the last few weeks. Realizing that light was but a figment, just a mirage of hope, the wall now crumbled and all the pain and torment and guilt came tumbling down, wracking her body in great waves of anguish. Samantha hugged her knees to her chest. A long, high-pitched wail that seemed to originate from the pit of her stomach escaped from her lips and grew in volume until it became a bellow of such sorrowful agony, the alien shrank from her in confusion.

Samantha wept unrestrained on the wooden deck while the alien stared at her dumbfounded. He stole a baleful glance at the satchel Matron Salek had given him, but did not turn to fetch it. Instead, he allowed Samantha to weep.

Later he carried her to one of the rooms and laid her gently on a bed with the covers drawn back. He took off her shoes, but left her tunic on and pulled the covers over her shaking shoulders.

After a while, utterly exhausted, Samantha drifted off. Later she dreamed she was back in her woods, hunting rabbits for breakfast. She smiled with glee and excitement, talking to herself about her family's reaction when she brought home fresh meat. She discovered a rabbit just inside its burrow and pulled the string of her bow taut, aligning the shaft perfectly with the rabbit's head. But as she released the bolt, the rabbit disappeared. Samantha jumped up, certain she had hit it, only to find Kimberley's lifeless body and the arrow lodged in her little sister's heart.

THE SUN STREAMED THROUGH SAMANTHA'S BEDROOM WINDOW when she woke. Dust motes danced in the rays of sunshine that lanced the room. For a moment she felt disorientated, not sure about time or place. She rubbed her eyes. They were dry and crusty from sleep and old tears. Her throat hurt. As she got out of bed, memory of the previous day rushed back, and a heaviness pressed down on her.

But Samantha would not cry. The dam broke yesterday, but she wouldn't allow it to break again. She was empty now and had no more tears to give. Besides, whatever happened to her from here on out, she deserved it. Hope was too dangerous a thing to hold on to.

She stepped from the room and saw a long hall leading to a stairway. The floor was carpeted and soft and felt strange under her feet. Downstairs, she found Master Zocht at the dining room table. He smiled at her as she descended.

"I've news for you, Bol. Great news, in fact. I located your sister."

Samantha wasn't sure if she had heard correctly, or whether this was yet another cruel twist of fate meant to punish her somehow.

"Kimberley...?" Her sister's name felt thick on her tongue.

"Well, yes, but her name is not Kimberley, anymore. Like you, she has been given a new name. She is now called Sand."

Samantha's lips moved, but no sound came out. She sat down abruptly on the bottom stair, her legs suddenly incapable of carrying her weight. She was speechless.

"I don't want you to worry. Sand is well. Another family has taken her in as a companion for their own daughter who is of similar age."

"Can I see her?" Samantha blurted out.

"Not yet. Hopefully, in time, we can work something out." Master Zocht smiled. "Aster Radek Guttor is head of the family. He is *larie* caste and occupies a senior position within the leadership. Due to the nature of his responsibilities, he has been relocated to an island off the coast of Auckland. Only a selected few inlari have clearance to visit the island, and, as such, it is best we wait for an opportune moment once he returns with his family to Auckland."

Master Zocht also explained that, because of the secretive nature of Master Guttor's work on the island, a moratorium on any and all communication had been put in place. Even he did not know the nature of the work being done there. "Just know she is safe and well taken care of," he continued and motioned for Samantha to join him. "You must be famished. Come have some breakfast."

Fresh tears rimmed Samantha's eyes. *So much for being empty,* she thought. At least Kimberley was alive. And if she was alive, there was hope to escape this wretched place. It was the first good news she had heard since the day the aliens had taken them. The sunlight slicing through the spacious living room suddenly seemed like rays of gold, and Samantha smiled.

Hope was alive after all.

THE NEXT COUPLE OF WEEKS DRAGGED ON, EACH DAY FEELING LIKE a year to Samantha as she harassed Master Zocht for news of her sister. He was patient with her and continued to explain that it was too early—that he would need to establish a relationship first with the family—and that Sand needed time to settle into her new routine. He assured Samantha her sister was safe, though, and that they were kind to Sand. These assurances, and knowing that, for now, at least, her sister was out of harm's way, allowed Samantha to relax more, and a fragile peace settled in her subconscious. It allowed her to focus on her studies, which, as time passed, increased in volume and intensity.

Samantha's daily routine consisted of cleaning the house in the mornings, which at first appeared daunting due to the size of the house, but she got used to it rather quickly, and, in due course, keeping it clean and tidy required minimal energy and time. The afternoons were allocated to study of inlari culture and history. She learned Master Zocht was *larie* caste, and the aliens' version of an anthropologist, and that he was tasked by the leader of Lakarta, *Madeer* Valnia Alteiri herself, to prepare a report on human nature.

Master Zocht's decision to do a hands-on experiment in secret acted as catalyst for the bond that began to form between Samantha and him. It allowed her to trust him more easily. After all, not once did he use the collar to discipline her, not even after she broke a plate, or when she cracked one of the data screens that lined the walls of his home. Instead, he reprimanded her like a parent would, sending her to her room without dinner. Other times, he would take away special luxuries and privileges. One of those luxuries was movies made by humans from before the Great Inlari War. The movies were in English and linked Samantha to a past that was unknown to her. It showed humans free and happy, with bountiful resources, a utopian past she was desperate to hold on to.

She still missed her parents terribly and felt their absence, most notably at night in bed, when the moon was full and bright and threw its light shimmering across the Pacific Ocean. She would stare at the brilliant sphere and wonder whether her parents could see her, and sometimes she would talk to them, imagining that they were there, shrouded by the moon's light, watching over her. During these conversations, Samantha would make promises of returning home one day with her sister to rebuild their cabin. It brought a peace to her nights, and after a while she became convinced her parents watched over her and Kimberley.

News from the other family had only been good. Her sister

was adapting nicely, and it made Samantha feel less guilty about the pleasure she derived from everyday things.

One of her daily lessons focused on inlari society, the norms and societal rules, the caste system, and the obligations of each inlari.

"It doesn't seem fair," Samantha responded one day after an inlari etiquette lesson. "I mean, it's so unfair to treat someone as if they have less value than you."

Master Zocht smiled patiently, like he usually did, before responding. "You have to remember, little one, this system has been part of the inlari fiber for thousands of years, if not millions. It fosters a balance and follows a philosophy that each inlari is born for a select purpose. Nothing less and nothing more. And so, each inlari, from birth, is honed and trained to function and operate within the paradigm of whatever position or rank has been selected for him or her. It works. It makes for a functioning society that is productive and brings about advancement across many fields. And, you have to remember that, if you know nothing else except the inlari way, then our system seems perfect and fair."

"I suppose so." Samantha shrugged. "But what if it's wrong anyway?"

Master Zocht laughed. "Oh my dear Bol. It is all relative. I've taught you about the inlari culture, and I have taught you about the different human cultures on Earth before we arrived. What is acceptable in one culture is not acceptable in another. Justice in one culture could be viewed as atrocity or injustice in another. There are no absolutes in life except time. Not even death is the final step."

And so it went, week after week. Master Zocht and Samantha would either sat by the dining room table or outside in the garden, with its magnificent views of the harbor and surrounding areas, or else in his study, in front of a line of multicolored screens, where he allowed Samantha access to his information archives. He taught her to write and read the inlari language, Anshahar, and at first it troubled her, but once she understood the logic behind the sounds and signs, she easily progressed.

He taught her about the Great Star, Inlar, who, it is said, created the first inlari nation and would one day reclaim them from the enemy that hunted them. This great evil was known as Rordorah, the Black Star, the Planet Eater and Taker of Life. Other than that, Master Zocht was quite vague when speaking of Rordorah or its mindless minions, the boleeron. He did not expand on their nature or appearance. Samantha saw fear in his eyes when he spoke of them and decided not to push the subject.

Samantha was allowed to grow out her hair, which she was thankful for. Having long hair again reminded her of a time when her mom used to plait her hair and fuss over her. It was a small reminder of a time that seemed from another life.

There was safety and peace in having a daily routine, and with the promise of being united with her sister one day, the throb of loss became dull and distant.

Her collar was replaced each year to allow for growth in her size. Because the collar could only be unlocked at the detention center, Master Zocht had to take her back there, where Matron Salek would fit a new one. Still unsmiling and curt, Matron Salek seemed unchanged by time.

On her twelfth birthday, Samantha saw Carik again at the detention center. Master Zocht had taken her for a collar replacement when she saw Carik exit Matron Salek's office. Her master was a tall inlari male with fat, stubby horns and jowlish cheeks, clad in a woven robe of deep red and gold trim. A ripple of ice ran down Samantha's spine when she saw his eyes. Beads of dark menace set in browless sockets leered at her.

Samantha stepped in closer to Master Zocht, who must have felt her fear, for he placed his arm around her shoulders. She shuddered.

"Greetings Drankel," Master Zocht said in Anshahar, breaking the silence and forcing the other to focus on him and respond in kind. Although Samantha could not yet speak the language fluently, she knew enough to follow the conversation.

"Greetings, Zocht. By the Great Star, you have a fine *bellogan* there with you."

"Inlar has blessed me, yes. Bol is an efficient housekeeper and prepares the best meals in all of Lakarta."

Drankel sniffed and gave a half sneer as he studied Samantha. She felt the intensity of his stare, like his eyes were drilling into her soul. "Yes, indeed, Zocht," he said slowly, "It seems I have not been granted the same fortune."

He reached back and grabbed Carik by the arm, pulling her roughly next to him.

Samantha was shocked at Carik's appearance. Her white-blond hair was tied in a severe ponytail that ordinarily would have accentuated her features, only it didn't now. It highlighted the bruises and scars on her face. She had lost the youthful excitement Samantha remembered. Carik's iceberg-colored eyes were now watery and tepid. Dull. Her gaunt face bore multiple bruises in different stages of fading. An old scar twisted from her upper lip, leaving her mouth in a permanent snarl.

"My *bellogan* does not cook, of course." Drankel licked his lips as he stroked Carik's head. "But she is useful in other ways, many other ways." He gave a short laugh. "Although, I fear she might be getting worn out, and then what do I do?" His eyes lingered on Samantha as he said the words. Carik's expression did not change, and she remained silent; her vacant gaze saw nothing and no one. "Ah! I hear a new consignment of *bellogans* arrives next week." Drankel continued, "I might send this one to the Island if the quality is good."

Samantha saw anger flash in Master Zocht's eyes, but he remained quiet. Master Drankel was well within his rights to treat a slave in any manner he deemed fit.

"I would love to continue our discussion, Drankel, but time is against us. I have an appointment. May Inlar bless you with just rewards. You make all inlari so proud."

Drankel stiffened at the poorly veiled sarcasm but said nothing. Instead, a smile formed on his broad face. "And you, Zocht. And you."

That night Samantha could not sleep. Her thoughts were filled with Carik's tortured face and the unspeakable cruelty she must endure daily at the hands of that monster. There was nothing she could do for her; neither could Master Zocht. She had already pleaded with him, but he had told her he was powerless to do anything. Master Drankel was elite. Zocht was *larie*.

Reuniting with Carik had reminded Samantha that Lakarta was a dangerous place for humans.

FOR HER FOURTEENTH BIRTHDAY, MASTER ZOCHT PROMISED Samantha a trip to the city center. Apart from exchanging her collar at the detention center once a year, Samantha had not ventured anywhere else and led an isolated existence. Her only link with the outside world was the digital information archive that Master Zocht allowed her to study. She had grown into a tall and lean young woman, and with her obsidian-colored hair and dark eyes, she posed a striking figure.

Samantha had dressed in a spotless white tunic with a tan undervest and new white canvas shoes for the trip. The soles were rubber and comfortable, but Samantha gave them no second thought. Fashion, after all, was of no consequences to someone in her position.

Excitement pulsed through her as she thought of the looming day trip. And yet, fear of the unknown—of venturing into a place that harbors only animosity—tempered her mood. Though Master Zocht had assured her that if she stayed by his side and obeyed the rules, she would have nothing to fear, Samantha still felt a jolt in the pit of her stomach—not unlike what it must feel like to step into a den of lions.

She had yet to unite with Kimberley, who would now be the same age Samantha was when they were kidnapped. Although her need to reconcile with her sister still drove her thoughts and haunted her nights, Samantha had grown used to a life of structured routine, and guarantees from Master Zocht that Kimberley was doing fine, and that they would eventually unite, sustained her. She had grown to trust her alien teacher.

Samantha studied herself in the mirror while she plaited her hair. She was a human girl learning alien things in an alien place surrounded by aliens. What chance did she have of ever escaping? Maybe that is why she had come to accept her own lot. Maybe that was why—

"Bol!" Master Zocht's voice broke her reverie. "Come down quickly!"

Surprised, Samantha called from her room. "I'm almost ready Master Zocht. You're early."

Master Zocht had gone to work that morning like any other morning, but he had planned to return in the afternoon to pick Samantha up for the trip to the city. Samantha looked at the tablet on her bedside table. It was still early morning. He had been gone scarcely an hour.

"Forget about the trip. Come down. There is something I need to tell you. Hurry, girl!"

In the five years she'd been living in his house, she had never heard him speak like that, not with this edge of panic to his voice.

Curious, Samantha jumped up, her slender fingers hastily tying the last loose tresses as she hurried to the stairway.

She saw Master Zocht pacing frantically in the entrance hall. His usual lighthearted face was knotted with concern and panic.

"Master Zocht, what's wrong?" Samantha asked as she came down the stairs.

Master Zocht's face was pure misery. "They deceived me, Bol. They...they lied to me. I'm so sorry. By the Great Star, I am so sorry."

"Master Zocht, you're scaring me!" Panic started to set in. "What are you talking about? Lied about what? Who?" Samantha's heart hammered in her chest. She had never seen him like this, and it frightened her.

"Your sister..." Master Zocht began, "she is—"

A loud crash shattered the moment, and three Parhata stormed through the wide front door into the entrance hall.

"How dare you!" Master Zocht began, but he was butted in the face by the lead officer. He fell to the floor, blood running down his shattered nose.

"Secure the traitor," the officer snapped, "and the *bellogan*."

In that one moment, Samantha was nine-years-old again, and an almost forgotten fear rushed back and surged through her like a tidal wave of horror. She gasped and sat down where she stood, her legs too weak to hold her up.

The soldiers were clothed in black tunics with red trim, and each carried a blaster as a sidearm on his hip. One of the officers approached her and hauled her up by the hair. Samantha gasped from the pain and grabbed at his hands. He shook her and she yelped. The pain was excruciating. It felt like the alien was tearing her hair from her scalp. The officer pulled her towards the front door; caught off balance, her legs dragged behind her on the tiled floor.

"This is unnecessary! How dare you touch me or my *bellogan*!" Master Zocht was on his knees, supporting himself on his arms when he spoke. Blood ran freely down his face and pooled on the tiled floor. "You have no authority to enter my domicile and abuse me like a common *bellogan*. Do you know who I am?"

"Oh, but we do. Traitors have no rights." The lead officer grinned. "But you know that."

"What are you talking about?" Master Zocht sat up now and pulled a handkerchief from within his tunic. He dabbed at the blood trickling from his nose.

"Keep your mouth shut, traitor. You'll have time to explain soon enough."

The third soldier produced two metal bracelets that he clasped around Master Zocht's wrists and pushed closed. A tiny blue light flashed on the one, followed by a dull clunk, and Master Zocht's wrists were secured by the electromagnetic handcuffs.

The leader brutally kicked him in the face, and he fell backwards.

Samantha screamed and tried to dislodge the soldier's hold on her hair. "Stop! What are you doing? Master Zocht has done nothing wrong! Please, leave him alone!" She pleaded with them in Anshahar, but the soldier holding her just yanked her away and continued outside, where he bundled her into the back of a bulky black six-wheeled vehicle. "Where are you taking me?" Samantha asked, her voice small and fragile.

"Keep quiet!" The officer spat and slammed the door shut. Through the back window, she saw Master Zocht, flanked by two soldiers, exit the house. They held him by his arms as he tottered unsteadily between them. His face was a bloody mess. They pushed him headfirst into the back of the second vehicle and shut the door, then signaled the driver of Samantha's vehicle to go, while they went back inside the house.

Fear blazed in Samantha's mind and seized her body in an icy grip. Master Zocht looked dispirited as he sat in the vehicle, chin on his chest. He must have felt Samantha's eyes on him, because he lifted his head and smiled at her. The smile was weak and miserable. Samantha saw great sadness on his ruined face. Master Zocht's lips formed the word "sorry" as Samantha's vehicle accelerated out of the driveway, away from the place she had called home for the last five years.

ELECTRICITY SURGED THROUGH SAMANTHA'S BODY IN HEATED waves, contorting her limbs as muscles spasmed and jerked. Then it mercifully stopped, leaving her useless on the floor, sucking in mouthfuls of air into screaming lungs. Her muscles ached and burned, and she tried to lie as still as possible, for each movement brought fresh agony to her battered body. Her heart shuddered wildly and felt like it was boring a hole through her ribcage.

"Get up!" The voice barely registered in Samantha's consciousness, so focused was she on her misery. "Get up or taste another lesson." The voice belonged to the inlari officer who had assaulted Master Zocht.

"This will happen every time you lie to me. Do you understand, human?" In his hand he had the silver disk that operated Samantha's collar. "Now get up and sit down on that chair. Do it now."

Samantha sobbed, but she complied and crawled with difficulty to the chair. Her joints felt stretched and torn. With great effort she hoisted herself onto the chair. Her hair had been shorn off roughly, and dried blood from a half dozen cuts was visible on her stubbled head.

The aliens had taken her to a compound somewhere in the city. So she had at last seen the city, but she should have known it would not be under happy circumstances. They had brought her to this building, seemingly molded from a solid block of concrete, where they tossed her into a cell with only a metal bunk low against the one wall and a small hole in the corner to use as a toilet. The cell reeked of disinfectant and reminded her of the detention center. They came for her after a week, and then the interrogations started.

They had dragged her to a small sterile room containing only a metal chair. After two days, her clothes were stained by her blood and urine. They had beaten her, and she had pissed herself, and they had laughed.

And then they started using the discipline ring.

They kept asking her about Master Zocht, about what he

had told her and what her duties were at his house. Although she fully explained what she did—how he had taught her about inlaris, and how she taught him about human nature—they did not believe her. She told them he allowed her to watch movies made by humans, but they did not seem to care about that. They kept asking the same questions, and she gave the same answers. Sometimes she responded too slowly and a hand would split her lip as reward; or, a question would be whispered in her ear, the officer prodding the side of her head with his horns, and when she didn't answer, he would flick his head, and the horns would butt her hard enough to bruise her skin.

Samantha cried and whimpered and pleaded with them to stop, and somewhere during the interrogation she started calling for her dad. Something she hadn't done for years. At one stage, she saw her dad reaching out for her, and she laughed and tried to take his hand, but then a slap tore the image away, and she found herself back in the interrogation room.

ON THE THIRD DAY OF INTERROGATIONS, THEY ASKED HER ABOUT Aster Radek Guttor. They had given her a little water that morning, and Samantha had to pour it into her mouth because her lips were so bruised. The cold liquid stung her mouth and streamed down her chin.

A female inlari entered the room. She too was dressed in black with red trim. Her horns swept over her forehead and curved at the nape of her neck. The female's sharp cheekbones sported a bony ridge that curved around the eyes and melded with her horns. Her lips were thin and severe, her eyes so small Samantha could not determine their color—but then, her own eyes were swollen half shut, so she wouldn't have been able to see them clearly, anyway.

"What do you know about Aster Radek Guttor?" The alien showed Samantha the silver disk in her hand. The meaning was clear. She had better answer truthfully, and so Samantha did.

"My sister, Kimber...I mean Sand...had been placed with his family as playmate for their daughter. Master Zocht told me that. Please, just ask Master Zocht. Please don't hurt my sister. She didn't know I was looking for her. Please. She had nothing to do with my wanting to see her."

The inlari stared at Samantha with an odd expression and moved closer, placing her index finger underneath Samantha's chin, lifting it, inspecting her face closely.

"What did Zocht tell you about Aster Radek Guttor?" The alien's voice was almost a whisper.

"Nothing!" Samantha cried. "Just that he and his family live on an island because his work is secret; otherwise I would have united with my sister already." Fresh tears welled up in her eyes and poured over her bruised cheeks. "Please, I'm telling the truth." Her shoulders shook with fear and grief and pain, and the alien officer studied her for a long moment before stepping back and placing the silver disk back inside her tunic pocket.

"That was never a possibility. Your sister died during the first year of her captivity."

Samantha gasped.

Time froze.

Her heart skipped what felt like many beats. She had trouble breathing. "No, it's not true. Master Zocht said she was safe. We just had to wait until they came back to Auckland."

Samantha searched the alien's face for signs that all of this was just one big misunderstanding.

"Please, just ask Master Zocht!" Her words sounded feeble and desperate, and she knew it but didn't care. And yet, somewhere in the back of her mind, she must have suspected the truth. Maybe hope had blinded her, and maybe the truth was too painful for her to bear. Maybe she had created a reality where a happy ending awaited her and Kimberley. She shivered.

"No...No, it can't be. No..." Samantha shook her head, unwilling to accept what she knew must be the truth, but her words faltered. Her tortured mind could no longer carry the lie. The weight of it was too much.

An icy calmness descended on her. It flowed through her like water cutting through ice.

"How did she die?" Her voice was clear and unemotional when she looked up at the alien. There was no fear in Samantha's eyes. No pain. Just dark shiny pools of an undeterminable depth, and it caught the alien off-guard.

"It doesn't matter, *bellogan*. It's not important."

"It is important!" Samantha jumped up and faced the alien. "It's important to me," she said more softly, suddenly calm again. "Please, tell me."

Surprised, the alien had taken a step back. She took out the silver disk again, showing it to Samantha. "Sit down, *bellogan*," she hissed.

Samantha didn't sit down. She stared at the alien, unmoved by the threat. Her heart was still. Her thoughts calm. Nothing mattered now but the truth. "Please tell me what happened to my sister," she pleaded in a soft voice.

The alien didn't answer. Instead, she pressed the remote, and electricity surged through Samantha. She fell to the floor, jerking as the current moved cruelly through her body, but she made no sound and took her punishment silently.

AFTER A WEEK, THE *PARHATA* RETURNED SAMANTHA TO MASTER Zocht's home. The soldiers had searched the place and not in a kind way, but Master Zocht, who had been released three days prior, had taken time to clean the mess and restore his home to order. He had also requested a personal audience with *Madeer* Valnia Alteiri to fiercely and officially object to his treatment at the hands of the *Parhata*.

The aliens told Samantha nothing, except to say that the situation had been resolved. Her master would explain things to her if he deemed it necessary.

Master Zocht sat at the dining room table when Samantha arrived, a light blue smear of a bruise over the bridge of his thin nose—the only evidence of what had happened to him.

Samantha, on the other hand, bore all the signs of her ordeal. Being a slave for as long as she had meant she did not receive the healing serum. Unlike five years ago when they had use for her and wanted to teach her a lesson, they were done with Samantha now. Her bruised face and short hair contradicted the smooth lines of the house and its clean interior. She seemed the alien.

Master Zocht saw Samantha and jumped up, kicking the chair over in the process, and hurried towards her, his arms outstretched. "Oh my poor girl! What have they done to you?"

He tried to embrace her, but she jerked out of his arms and stepped back, her expression strained under the weight of her anger.

"I'm so sorry this has happened to you. They thought I was somehow spying for the humans." Master Zocht looked at her with a mixture of concern and shock.

"What happened to my sister?" Samantha's lower lip trembled as she waited for an answer.

Master Zocht let out a long breath and rubbed his face with both hands, and then, lowering his hands, he said, "Sand—"

"Kimberley! Her name is Kimberley!" Samantha snapped.

"I apologize," Master Zocht said quickly, realizing the dramatic change in Samantha. He continued more carefully, "Your sibling... Kimberley, was taken to The Great Barrier Island. That part was true, but she was never part of Guttor's family. She was a test subject used in his experiments. I'm so sorry, Bol." Master Zocht's face was etched with sorrow.

"I have no idea what the nature of the experiments were, or, precisely, what kind of scientist Guttor is." Master Zocht continued. "All I know now is that she perished within the first year she was there. That is what they told me."

Samantha showed no reaction to the news, but her face was pale now. She stood there, impassively, her eyes shining like obsidian glass, hate and anger writhing and coiling under the surface like serpents readying to strike. The transformation shocked Master Zocht. His mouth opened and closed again.

"Why now? After so many years, why now?" Samantha's voice was like ice, and she gave a step forward, her hands balled up into fists. She still wore her filthy tunic, stained by waste and blood. She had no shoes on, and her feet were black with grime.

Samantha had never seen an inlari cry. Although her experience with Master Zocht over the years meant she knew him very well and that excitement would spread to his face in an animated way when he was happy, his overall demeanor still bordered on stoic; and yet now, here in the entrance hall of his house in Half Moon Bay, in the aftermath of their terrible ordeal, Master Zocht wept silently.

"I wanted to surprise you, Bol. For your birthday. My intent was not to take you to the city, but to the island. I wanted you to see your sister." Master Zocht sobbed.

It was now Samantha's turn to be surprised, but she remained silent, her face a mask of impassivity.

"Every year I went to the ministry to ask for information about the Guttor family, and every year they gave me the same answer: That due to security precautions, no one was allowed to enter the island. No other information was forthcoming. But this year I filed a special request to visit the island." Master Zocht wiped the tears from his eyes with the palms of his hands. "I guess my frequent requests must have raised suspicion. They use the island to experiment on humans. It is horrible. I did not know. Bol, by the Great Star, I did not know."

Samantha felt a sudden urge to give him comfort, to let him know she believed him, but she could not force herself to act. A terrible anger burned inside of her. It was dark and furious and unwavering.

"I need to leave this place," she said bluntly. "Lakarta, I mean. This isn't my home."

Master Zocht stammered, "But you can't, Bol. It's impossible."

"I don't have a choice. I can't stay here anymore." Rage flared in her eyes. "They murdered my sister and parents. I want to kill all of them. Every last one!" The words came out in a rush of bitterness.

"Every last one, Bol? Even me?" Master Zocht stared at her,

his eyes still wet, shock etched on his face. "Even me?" He asked again, this time softly.

Samantha ignored his question. "Will you help me escape?"

"Oh, Bol...I can't...I don't know how. What about your collar? It can only be deactivated at the detention center. And even if you somehow managed to do that, how will you travel back to Australia? A submersible? A fishing boat? They monitor the waters, dear girl. And what about me? If I help you, they will kill me this time."

"If you won't help me, I'll leave anyway." Samantha's lips were set in grim determination. Something cold had settled in her during her time in that stinking cell. She knew she would die if she stayed here any longer. Her mind was a storm of guilt and hate, and now anger fueled the flames of that hate, and it was a consuming thing that had overtaken all her other emotions.

"Please," Master Zocht begged. "Don't go. Give me a day or two to think about this. Your room is ready for you. I know you are tired. I can see it. Go rest, Bol. Give me time to search for options."

Samantha's face softened for a moment, and she saw the pain on Master Zocht's face. *Probably the only human alien alive,* she thought. A great exhaustion overcame her then. She smiled. It was a tired smile, and she embraced Master Zocht at last. It made him weep again as he folded his arms around her. But there were no tears from Samantha, for she felt nothing except a lassitude that settled in her bones and made her head ache. And so she turned and went up the stairs to her room, fell on her bed, and was soon asleep.

SAMANTHA SLEPT THE REST OF THE DAY AND THROUGH THAT NIGHT, waking early the next morning. Her eyes felt like they had sand in them, and her head was groggy. A light flickered on her tablet next to her on the bedside table, indicating a message waited for her. She checked it. Master Zocht had gone to work early and requested that she take it easy and not do anything rash. He asked her to wait for him. He had a plan. The message was an hour old.

Samantha sank back into her pillows and closed her eyes. She saw the faces of her family, of her mom and dad, of her little sister. She saw them as they were back then, happy and smiling. For so many years she had busied herself with thoughts of her sister—how she would look, what she would be doing, whether she liked the same food, and whether she was happy—and Samantha imagined how her face must be changing and wondered if her dimples would disappear or remain and whether her hair color would change. But now the nightmare truth had been revealed that her sister never even saw her fifth birthday. The aliens took her life, and they did so in the cruelest of ways.

Samantha's throat became thick with emotion, and she felt a sharp ache in her chest, but she willed the tremulous thoughts back down and locked them up deep inside her where no one would ever have access. She stared at the white ceiling and listened to the birds singing and chirping outside, the far-off low hum of traffic in that hated city, and the noises in the port below. Somewhere a dog barked, and the world sounded normal. How strange then, she thought, that such normalcy hid such evil. The aliens were an abomination. They did not fit with nature. They affected the balance of things. She now knew there was purpose to her life. That she had been made to endure such harsh cruelty by the hands of these scum for a reason. They had taken everything from her.

And she would take everything from them. This would be her life's mission. Once she got back to Australia, she would travel to Queensland and join her dad's unit.

Samantha dozed for an hour more before she got up. She peeled off her dirty clothing and showered, pulling on a fresh tunic and pants before she went downstairs for breakfast.

IT TOOK ALMOST A MONTH, BUT MASTER ZOCHT MANAGED TO FIND a fishing boat to smuggle Samantha over the Tasman Sea to Victoria. But they had to travel all the way to the other side of Lakarta to a small town on the southwestern coast called, Opunake. The port there consisted of a single half-rotted jetty, and the inlari presence in the area was minimal. Master Zocht knew a like-minded colleague who owned a fishing trawler, though he used humans to skipper the boat and fish the seas. This was a strange arrangement, and the details were vague. There were also rumors that inlaris and humans coexisted peacefully in Victoria, and so Opunake, being only about 2,500 km from Victoria, made the most sense. She did not know the details of how Master Zocht had managed to get a boat or a willing skipper, and she didn't care. She was going back home.

It felt sad leaving Master Zocht, who had been kind to her and who, in his own way, loved her, but Samantha felt no emotional tie, or if she did, it was lost somewhere in the tangled mess of her soul. He was the enemy. Only, he did not act like the enemy, and he had been there during her formative years as she grew under his tutelage. That just made things more complicated. A part of her loved him, she was certain of that. Because of him she hadn't suffered Carik's fate, or worse. Because of him she was able to escape New Zealand.

And escape she did. It was remarkably simple to orchestrate, once the boat had been secured. Master Zocht would certainly get into trouble when they discovered his slave had gone AWOL. There would be questions, maybe even an interrogation to understand how she had managed to remove her collar without the detention center's knowledge and without it blowing her head off. But Master Zocht would simply explain his judgment had been defective. That he never thought Bol would flee. He would tell them how he had treated her kindly, and she had given him no reason to suspect betrayal. He would also explain how he had obtained special permission for Bol to travel to Wellington to accompany him when he delivered his speech on *The Nature of the Human Species*, a project he had been working on for many years. He was scheduled to appear in front of a gaggle of fellow scholars at a symposium on *The Human Problem*.

Of course, the range was too great for the collar to work effectively, and he had secured a special release order, so Samantha's discipline ring had been removed. That was the only way for her to travel to Wellington safely and without incident. He would, of course, explain his embarrassment at what happened and how he feared his professional and scientific credibility may have suffered because of his slave's betrayal.

In the end, however, Master Zocht's status would save him from any permanent harm to either his career or his health, and he would continue his work unabashed.

She watched as Master Zocht waved goodbye from the dark rocky shore, a solitary figure on a half-rotten jetty, looking uncomfortable and out of place. Samantha did not respond and watched as Master Zocht grew smaller and smaller, until he was a mere speck on the moving horizon.

Waves crashed against the bow as the trawler pushed forward towards Victoria. Samantha stood outside the wheelhouse, enjoying the surf spray on her skin and the cool sea breeze playing through her hair.

She was going home. She was going home!

THE FISHING TRAWLER WAS AN OLD MESS OF FLECKED PAINT AND rusted metal, and it reeked of rotting fish. It was called *The Merry Sue*, and her skipper was a free human male named Torry, who traded fish to the inlari.

Under his fisherman's cap, Torry's face was like tanned leather creased too many times. He was thick-shouldered, and tattoos decorated his muscular forearms. His filthy beard hid a cruel mouth, and his flat nose spoke of too many bar-room brawls. Torry's piggish eyes had stripped Samantha to the bone the moment he saw her board his rust bucket. She should have been afraid, but she just shot him a baleful glance.

A bank of dark cloud rumbled low over them, turning the moody seas a dark cyan. *The Merry Sue* fought the rising swells as the sea breeze grew stronger and turned into icy gales.

"Hey, missy, you'll catch a cold standing out there like that. Come join me here!" Torry shouted from the wheelhouse.

Samantha ignored him, but the cold wind cut through her and she shivered. She turned and ascended the bridge ladder, tossing her small backpack into the corner.

The wheelhouse stank of sweat and urine and old food, and it looked as grimy as it smelled.

Torry leered at her, his beady eyes shiny. He seemed not to have noticed Samantha's scowl or the clear revulsion in her face.

"Why don't you come closer, lass. Ol' Torry'll keep you warm." He reached out to her with his calloused right hand, but Samantha slapped it away.

Torry gave a short laugh and shook his head. "You don't want to be playing hard to get, missy. You'll only get hurt that way."

Samantha didn't say a word and glared at him. A calm rage simmered behind her eyes.

"The way I see it, girl, you have two choices here. You can fight me and lose, and then I'll give you back to the boneheads. Or," Torry licked his lips, "you can just go with it, and I'll have you in Port Albert come morning. What's it gonna be, girl?"

To emphasize her non-choice, Torry lifted his thick jersey, and Samantha saw a short knife with a curved blade riding his hip in a leather sheath.

Samantha shuddered at the thought of what this guy wanted from her—what he wanted to take from her by force. So much had already been taken from her.

No more.

Samantha dove forward, reaching out as if to grab the knife on Torry's hip. Instinctively, he jumped back, his hand automatically reaching for it, but the knife was not Samantha's intended target. Next to the ship's wheel, where Torry had stood just a moment ago, sat a tin cup steaming with dark liquid. Samantha swept the cup up and into Torry's face. He yelped and swore and clawed at his face as the scalding-hot liquid burned him. Samantha shoved him back and plucked his knife from its sheath, but instead of jumping back, she attacked him. The silver blade glinted dully as it sliced down into Torry's groin. The fisherman's hands shot down, and he grabbed his balls, exposing his face to Samantha. Again she sliced down, twice, crisscrossing Torry's face, cutting it to the bone.

He fell back and lay crumpled on the floor of the wheelhouse, bleeding and sobbing.

Something dark had snapped in Samantha. She felt no pity and stared at the pathetic wretch in front of her.

"Please, no more," he pleaded, blood drooling from his torn lips. "I meant no harm."

"Meant no harm?" Samantha's voice was colder than the icy gale outside. She wheeled around and grabbed the fourteen-inch priest hanging by a leather loop under the ship's wheel. "And I *do* mean you harm." She raised the club just as lightning crackled outside, illuminating the wheelhouse's interior. Torry screamed as the club came down in a sickening thud, again, and again, and again.

Nature has a way of reclaiming everything.

It had been nine months since her escape from New Zealand. She would never call it Lakarta again. Samantha stood where her family's cabin used to rest. Where once a wisp of smoke trickled lazily from the chimney, and where sounds of laughter came as naturally as the birdsong outside.

Bush and weed had now overtaken the site, and here and there she could still see charred pieces of plank and cabin that had been burned to stumps jutting from between the tall grass, and broken beams rotting in the soil. The chimney wall remained, standing guard over the ruins of the cabin, though crumbling and in a state of imminent collapse.

Samantha had dug through the rubble, hoping to find at least some sign of her parents, maybe their skeletal remains, so she could give them a decent burial, but she found nothing. Or maybe they were buried too deep. If that was the case, then this site would serve as a fitting grave. She had already gone to the woods, high up the slope where the berserker had chased her all those years ago. She had searched for her knife and, by some miracle, she had found it. Time had hidden the knife under dirt and leaf mold. The blade was rusted, but she would clean it and, hopefully, still salvage the steel. One day she'd find those aliens who had murdered her family and use the blade on them. The thought made her smile.

But here she stood now, familiar soil underneath her booted feet, a cool breeze blowing down the Barren Mountain, pushing her damp shirt against her scarred back, surrounded by the incessant natter of lonely cicadas calling to their mates.

It was her homecoming song, and it was beautiful.

THANK YOU

If you enjoyed this book, we'd love to hear from you.

Consider leaving us a review on your favorite websites:
Amazon
Kobo
Goodreads

We're counting on you.
Thank you for reading and for your support.

AUTHORS

M. J. Kelley is a short fiction aficionado, writer of speculative fiction, and humorist with a passion for education. He's fond of fog and can peel a carrot with a look. M. J. dwells in San Francisco, CA, seasonally as well as year round.

Dana Leipold loves the written word. Her award-winning debut novel, *Burnt Edges*, delves into the dark reaches of abuse and incest while depicting the resilience of one young girl. She practices yoga, loves funny cat videos, and lives in the San Francisco Bay Area with her husband and two children.

Woelf Dietrich mostly writes tales of dark fantasy and the supernatural, which is maybe not such a far cry from his lawyering days. Sometimes he writes other things. He resides in New Zealand with his wife and kids and a dog.

Elaine Chao is obsessed with a number of things, including languages, storytelling, martial arts, music, geeking out, psychology, software, event management, design, and her two cats. At any given point in time, you can find her doing two out of ten in the San Francisco Bay Area.